BIG NIGHT OUT

Lesbian Adventure Series Stories

Tex Star

www.treeboundtreasures.com

All of my books are dedicated to
Love and Life
... I hope you find yours.

LASS : Lesbian Adventure Series Stories

The Lesbian Adventure Series Stories are a collection of short stories except you do not read from cover to cover. As in life there are decisions to be made: from basic questions about what underwear to put on: to the bigger questions about whether to seduce the whole soccer team. Written to be fast paced, the stories are designed to take you on an amazing journey using your imagination as the guide, for throughout each story, you are in control. Whether you choose a safe route or whether you are daring, there is guaranteed to be a surprising outcome. These are the sliding doors of life and as with life, anything can happen. Just remember, that if you make an opposite decision, it does not mean you have an opposite outcome.

Whether travelling on a bus, or relaxing on a beach, this series is specifically designed for those who like quick adventurous reads. Based on the decisions made, each story can potentially be brief or multi-layered. Thus, in one book, you have the potential to read it over and over with a guaranteed different outcome every time. Each book holds twenty or more endings and a myriad of ways to reach them. As a special bonus, there is a secret ending in each book for those of you who are the most curious.

Reading a LASS Book

Starting on the first page, the idea of the story is set out. At the bottom of each section is an option to choose to continue the story. Each choice refers to a specific chapter number. Skip to that chapter to continue the story. Your story, your choices, your personal journey. Enjoy!

TRUE FACT

Life is a book of possibilities, just like this one. You just have to be brave enough to turn the page.

1

Wow, what a long month. Breaking up with your cheating girlfriend was the toughest part. It hurt, and though you've been acting fine about it you are still bewildered inside. It felt like it came out of the blue, but looking back over the last few months, you have to admit there were a few signs.

As you both wanted to buy a house, her working later and longer seemed worthwhile. Sure, it took a toll on the relationship, but you had convinced yourself it was only a short-term hiccup. Now, the fact that she dressed nicer for work, and took more private work calls at home, are glaring alarms. The goal justified the means. The goal was a happy future together. A secure future.

A goal. Yes, a goal seemed a good idea three months ago. It was a goal worth forfeiting your dream job for one less enjoyable but better paying. Minor sacrifices for a lifetime together. It all seemed worthwhile. Now you were flush with cash but had no goal, no girlfriend, no direction, no future. Your best friend

Maddie just rang to encourage you, no, force you, to go clubbing tonight.

So here you are standing in front of the mirror, trying on your sixth shirt. Did it give the right look? Would any give the right look? To be honest you didn't know what look you were after. Maddie said you needed to get laid. Did you want that? Was it even an option? Why not? A smile grows on your face, it's the first in a month. Freedom is yours, and the club will be your playground.

Turning the music louder you rip the conservative shirt from your shoulders. Your bra looks conservative too. Removing it, you do a little jig, your butt swaying to the music. Looking in the mirror you consider underwear options.

Do you choose to stay in your boxers?
Turn to 16
Do you choose to put on your Smurf underwear?
Turn to 87
Do you choose to put on a French G-string?
Turn to 96

2

You approach the red head. It has been so long since you've made a move. Surely it hasn't changed that much? Stopping two seats short of her, you sit down and order a drink. Then another for courage. Someone else approaches and speaks to her. Laughter bubbles from her mouth. Cursing that you may have lost your moment, you smack the bar in frustration.

Looking sulkily into your drink a hand appears next to yours. The well-manicured nails are short. The fingers, slender and long. You wonder if they belong to a piano player. As you raise your eyes, the woman speaks.

'Can I buy you a drink?'

It is the red head.

'That would be delightful.'

You stammer, now unsure of how this dance continues. Once again laughter bubbles from her mouth. You imagine the bubbles, feeling them fall about you. The image makes you smile. The woman introduces herself as Ginger, and you can't imagine her name being anything else.

Ginger comments on how cute you are as she ruffles your hair. Accidentally her breasts brush against your ear. Is that her heart or yours that you can hear? The smell of her perfume is intoxicating.

After ruffling your hair once again, she lowers her lips to your ear. The warmth from her mouth seeps into your skin. Her breath tickles as she speaks.

'Want to come home with me?'

Do you choose to accept Ginger's offer?
Turn to 51
Do you choose to decline Ginger's offer?
Turn to 15

3

Moving to the sound of the music you glide towards the dance club. With a friendly smile the bouncer waves you in. The room is full of sweaty bodies all moving to the music. Everyone is having fun rubbing against each other.

Checking out the possibilities, you glance up to see the DJ. Her name is DJX. Realising she is someone you know, you wave. She looks surprised but waves back in between music changes.

Loving the rhythm, you push your way to the front of the stage where the speakers are thumping so hard, they may topple. The music vibrates through your whole body and it feels exhilarating. You let the bass ravage you.

A girl next to you smiles. You smile back. She mouths hello as the music is momentarily suspended between a DJ change over. You mouth 'hi' for she is rather cute.

A wad of paper hits you in the head breaking your concentration. Looking up you see DJX waving and signalling to meet her at the side of the stage. You take another look at the cute girl. A second wad of paper hits you. This time DJX is giving you a stern look. The cute girl starts gyrating towards you.

Do you choose to stay on the dance floor?
Turn to 55
Do you choose to meet DJX?
Turn to 79

4

Grabbing another drink, you take in the time. The bus will arrive in a matter of minutes and since the club is only two stops away, it's the best option for a big night out. Proud of yourself for not drinking and driving, you slosh the drink in a salute before taking another swig.

Stepping out into the cool night, you walk the short distance to the bus stop. The well-lit bus arrives as scheduled. At this time of night, the bus looks like a fish tank glowing in a dark room. Its occupants, or lack of, can easily be seen through the glass windows. You pay the fair and look for a seat. The bus is almost empty except for a cute brunette sitting at the back. While staring in her direction you fail to notice as the bus jerks into motion. You temporarily lose your balance but grab a pole just in time not to fall flat on your face.

Looking up you see a smirk on the brunette's face. What a fantastic first impression. Slightly embarrassed for staring, the brunette turns away. You attempt to reconnect with a smile, yet her eyes focus on something outside the window.

Do you choose to sit at the rear of the bus?
Turn to page 80
Do you choose to remain standing at the front of the bus?
Turn to page 98

5

Running the red you feel rebellious. It's wrong, but justify the decision because you are running late. Besides, there are no other cars on the road. You look in your rear-view mirror and see nothing. Suddenly from behind an advertising billboard a police motorcycle appears. Red and blue lights are flashing and the siren is wailing. You swear under your breath.

Stopping, not far from the club, you hope no one sees you. Pulling up behind your car, the officer steps off the bike while removing their helmet. The shape of the body in tight leather says that it's a female officer. She swings her hair in the night breeze then places the helmet on the bike's seat. Right hand covering her gun she approaches your window. You have it wound down before she gets there. Your eyes are focused on the side mirror watching every step she takes. One of her hands rises to unzip her jacket a little. You lean closer to the mirror as she vanishes into your blind spot.

Suddenly, she is next to you, ducking towards the

open window. As you turn her bust comes into view. It is mere inches away. You are utterly absorbed with her breasts being held tightly by the leather jacket. With lustful hope, you want the zipper to fail, but it doesn't. It takes a moment before you can lift your eyes to hers. The words are a blur but you know she has got you for running the red.

Do you choose to flirt with the officer?
Turn to 48
Do you choose to accept the fine and proceed to the club?
Turn to 58

6

Ginger looks at you then the dong. Taking a step forward she snatches it from your hand.

'What do you think?'

Her words are sharp. She pushes you back until your shoulder blades are touching the cold shower screen. Goosebumps form on your skin.

'Turn around.'

Following the order, you wonder if Ginger is mad or being playful. Still confused, you are strangely willing to do as she commands. Your legs are trembling slightly.

'Drop them.'

Her hand is already at your waist, assisting you. Ginger, presses her breasts into your back, nibbles your ear, then in a forceful voice speaks again.

'Get in and set it to hot.'

Pushing herself away from your body, she slaps you on the arse with the dong.

'Now.'

You pause a moment. Your blood is racing. All of

this has taken you by surprise, yet you are very much stimulated by the situation. Turning on the shower taps, giving in to the unknown, you can't wait to see what will happen next.

END

7

Realistically you don't give a damn about the room service girl especially since you have the pressing matter of five near naked women in a hot steamy spa begging you to join them. They are splashing gleefully, begging you to return. It seems impossible to remove your focus from the spa, so you yell to the girl to tip herself from the jar.

The room service girl keeps her head down and sets a table right next to the spa. Taking her time but you don't notice. If you had, it would be reasonable to assume she was checking out the five naked woman, as were you. The table is filled with everything you could possibly want for a big night. Fresh berries with whipped cream. A bucket of semi melted ice cream. Chocolate topping and a squeeze bottle of honey. Not to mention the six chilled bottles of champagne.

Having everything at hand you jump into the spa fully clothed. This is not an issue as the girls claw the clothes from you amongst squeals of delight. Standing waist deep in water, it feels like an outer body experience, as these things only happen in movies. The water is warm as are their mouths on your skin.

Just as you are about to sink into the spa and the awaiting arms, lost in a sense of bliss, you feel the room service girl's presence at the edge of the spa staring at the six of you.

Do you ask the room service girl to join you?
Turn to 92
Do you tell the room service girl to leave?
Turn to 38

8

You turn down Millie's kind offer.

'How about dinner this week?'

You ask hopefully.

She smiles.

'Sorry but the band is starting a six-month tour of Europe.'

You feel a little distraught as she's an amazing person. Friends are lacking in your life, what with Maddie being vague with you and your ex claiming all your friends as hers. Truth is that she controlled your life so much that you had drifted away from your true friends years ago. As a couple all your friends were her friends.

As the timeline is tight you consider the options.

'How about dinner tonight?'

'Sounds wonderful!'

She gladly accepts. Millie appears to be as excited about it as are you. It's been a while since you've had dinner with anyone other than yourself, and even longer since you've had a decent conversation that didn't involve work.

Waiting by the stage till the set finishes, you dance to the beat. Running through your body the music makes you move in a way you never have before. This music rocks!

Before whisking Millie to your home, you help the band pack their van. They appreciate the assistance especially after such a hard set. The sweat pouring down their bodies shows how much they worked to put out a top performance. You wish them luck on their upcoming tour before heading off with Millie.

On the trip home, you marvel how incredible the band is. And how the music spoke to you. That you felt it in your soul. Millie's cheeks blush a little as she thanks you for the compliment.

Arriving home you offer Millie the use of your shower, as she is still sweat drenched. Gladly accepting the offer, she heads off with a clean towel. Standing alone in the kitchen you wonder what to make for dinner.

Do you choose to order in?
Turn to 39
Do you choose to cook something?
Turn to 46

9

Before you exit the cab you ask Cindy if she'd like a drink. Smiling, she looks you up and down.

'How about you join me at my motel for a drink. It's just around the corner. Besides, I'm not dressed for a club.'

You think about Maddie waiting inside for you. Maddie's aim for the night is for you to get out there again with a possibility of getting laid. You look at the club which is pumping. In the beer garden people are singing karaoke, while inside people are either at the bar listening to the jukebox or in the dance club dancing to a DJ.

Maddie is predictable, which means the night would hold little real surprise. Yes, the chance of getting laid is increased but so would the chance of getting into trouble. Cindy has a mysterious air about her. Maybe your chances would be lower with her, but by the look in her eyes you doubt it. Either choice holds a real chance of something.

Do you choose to accept the drink at Cindy's motel?

Turn to 70

Do you choose to decline and enter the club alone?

Turn to 58

10

From a previous experience, you have learnt to re-spect a person's privacy. Last time it totally didn't go in your favour, and you were left utterly embarrassed. Returning to the lounge room, Ginger is waiting for you in a fluffy gown.

'I hope you don't mind. It's a little more comfort-able.'

There is no issue with the gown, especially since it exposes plenty of flesh. Re-joining Ginger on the lounge, she moves closer, the warmth from her body makes your skin prickle. As she crosses her legs you sneak a glance at her silky inner thighs and imagine where they lead to. There is a desire to touch the skin but you resist. Ginger sees you looking so she leans even closer. Now her breasts come into view and they look even silkier.

You laugh weakly as Ginger inserts a grape into your mouth. The grape pops, dribbling juice from your lips. Ginger wipes it away with her finger. Placing the finger in her mouth she sucks it clean. The action is more stimulating than you think possible. You feed Ginger a grape and a little juice dribbles onto her lips. You lean forward and kiss it away. Ginger giggles softly, differently to the bubbly laugh you heard earlier. She invites you to the bedroom. Gladly you accept.

Taking you by the hand, Ginger leads you to the bed. Slowly she undresses you, placing kisses on each section of bare flesh that is revealed. The kisses tickle your skin. You try to reciprocate but she doesn't allow you. Nibbling here and there she ravages you passionately from every angle. You get lost in the ecstasy, enjoying every minute of her absolute attention. She makes you climax over and over. You are breathless but still wish to return the favour, yet Ginger only lets you kiss her breasts and stomach. As you search lower, she stops you.

Continue 11

11

'There's something I need to tell you.'

Returning your attention to her neck, you kiss her chin then her mouth as she tries to speak. Forcefully she pushes you from her. Ginger appears upset. It doesn't fit the moment. It confuses you.

'I need to tell you.'

You are slightly annoyed as you were both having a wonderful time, or at least you thought you were. Ginger is visibly upset, so you stop what you were doing. Wrapping your arm around her, trying to offer comfort, she starts to sob gently. Ginger's watery eyes look up into yours.

Her words are slow, withheld. She explains to you, her situation.

'I'm a transsexual – male to female. So far, I've only had breast surgery. I'm taking all the hormones. I've been saving for vaginoplasty, but it's been delayed by the psychologists.'

A look of disgust fills her face as she mentions the lower surgery. She withdraws from you.

'I feel incomplete, and ugly.'

Ginger explains further.

'I just wanted to spend some time with you, but you were so alluring I couldn't help myself. Was it bad that I wanted you so much?'

'No.'

You are flattered, though the situation is new to you. Your mind is rapidly sifting through the night's events.

Do you choose to leave immediately?

Turn to 41

Do you choose to stay with Ginger?

Turn to 78

12

You know it's wrong, very wrong, but you just have to look. While in the bathroom you explore Riley's medicine cabinet. Here you find testosterone blockers plus a myriad of other medications. Initially you are confused over their purpose. Stupidly you stand there reading each label. Unfortunately, you do not hear Riley enter the bathroom.

'I just wanted to see what was taking you so long.'

The voice was chipper until she saw what you were doing.

'How dare you!'

The words turned sharp. Sharper than you felt was needed for the situation. She slams the cabinet shut, nearly breaking your hand. Stunned, you look at her like a deer caught in headlights. Riley continues her rant as she leads you out of the room.

'I was going to tell you. It's just so hard.'

You still look at her bewildered. None of the medications made sense. It's not like you're a medical student or anything. You were just being nosey.

'Alright, alright. So, I'm a pre-op transsexual. I've had the top half done.'

Her eyes sink as if she is waiting for the right words from you.

'I'm sorry.'

Is all you can stammer yet she misinterprets this as you saying you want to bail on the situation. Riley leads you to the door and pushes you out. As it slams in your face you still feel confused. Tired from the night you decide to head home and try this getting laid thing another day.

END

13

All the charity work has made you tired. You apologise to Lucy and suggest you catch a movie another time. She's disappointed, stating she was enjoying your company. Her face lights up as she makes a suggestion.

'How about I call a cab and we drive out to the lake. I can borrow a blanket from the shelter, and we can sleep out on the shoreline till sunrise?'

Considering the offer, you respond.

'I do love a sunrise and I haven't seen one in the longest time.'

Your ex preferred clubbing over early starts, whereas you were the opposite. You love nature so the lake sounded awesome. Lucy took your words as a yes.

'It's settled then. I'll call us a cab.'

The cab drops you off in a secluded area by the water. Spreading out the blanket you both lie down starring skywards at the stars. Talking becomes less and less as you both drift off to sleep. You are jolted awake by Lucy who excitedly states the sun will be up shortly. She pulls a thermos from her bag and shares a cup of tea with you as the sun peaks over the horizon.

The rising sun chases the cool night air away as its warmth explodes over the lake. The glistening water stirs something inside of you. You can't recall the last time you saw a sunrise, nor can you recall someone being as excited about seeing one as you. Lucy is someone you want to get to know better. Fortunately, she wants to get to know you better too.

END

14

You lead the two girls outside with the intent of calling for a couple of uniforms to take them to the station. So as not to embarrass them in front of other club goers, you take them around the corner.

'What's your name?'

One asks. So you tell her.

'You're cute.'

The other says. You smile as you've heard it all before.

They plead with you not to book them because they are law students. You look doubtfully at them. One flicks her hair seductively, while the other sucks her finger, looking at you alluringly.

'Maybe we could do a trade. What do you like?'

They offer suggestions for their freedom, but you take your job seriously, so you refuse.

Jackie the bartender comes out the back door of the club which is further down the alley. She approaches to see what is happening. You fill her in once she says one of the girls is her younger sister.

After much discussion and as a favour to Jackie you let the two go with a very stern warning. They scoot back into the club.

You remain talking to Jackie who is killing time. Unbeknownst to either of you, Jackie's girlfriend comes from around the front of the building and sees you with her girl. Miscalculating the situation, she is so enraged, she covers the few metres in a couple of seconds and takes a swing at you. The punch lands hard on your left cheek. Jackie jumps into action grabbing her girlfriend and stopping her from throwing another punch. It takes a moment for Jackie to explain what the two of you were doing. Her girlfriend still looks unconvinced, even after seeing your badge, but apologizes anyway.

You decide to call it a night. Two black eyes are more than you wanted or needed.

END

15

Though you find Ginger quite stunning you decide not to accept her offer. There is just something about her that isn't quite right, but you don't seem able to put your finger on it. You thank her for the kind invitation.

She appears upset by your choice. Surprising you when she leans in and speaks in a very deep baritone voice.

'Do you have an issue with my kind?'

The voice, being so masculine, makes you naturally want to respond with 'no sir'. The situation is confusing, it makes your head hurt. Rubbing the pain you squint at the fine stubble on Ginger's chin.

Ginger takes the hint and leaves. You remain seated, totally stunned. Jackie the bartender gives you another drink though you haven't asked for one.

'Don't worry about Ginger. She's a psychologist conducting a survey on how gay people respond to transsexuals. Though by provoking people she'll get inaccurate results.'

You tell Jackie she seems to know a lot. She just shrugs her shoulders and says she sees a lot.

'I'm doing a PhD on a similar topic. Though I prefer my results to be unbiased so I study my subjects from a distance.'

You admit that would be better because the whole situation with Ginger confused you greatly. Jackie laughs.

Do you choose to keep drinking at the bar?
Turn to 49
Do you choose to enter the beer garden?
Turn to 61
Do you choose to enter the dance club?
Turn to 3

16

Boxers are awesome, especially for feeling the breeze, not to mention the easy access, if required. Hopefully it is required. You smile at yourself in the mirror, hands on hips, happy with your choice. Instead of dressing you move to the dresser to find the appropriate accessories.

Leather wrist strap and silver thumb ring are always a top choice. Followed by your guitar pick on a leather neck strap. Tonight, you feel like a rock star, ready to let loose. Maybe a few more rings, not for cosmetic value but if you go super wild, a fight might ensue, and they'll act like knuckle dusters.

Thoughts of your wild youth flashes through your head. Being tied down to one woman had changed you. You remove the clear piercing from your eyebrow and insert your favourite titanium rainbow ring with sharp ends. It fits and feels good, like meeting up with an old friend. Yes, this night is going to rock.

You check to see if the nipple rings still fit and let out a wild howl when, with some force, they do. You feel the old you re-emerging. The next choices are a no-brainer, firstly your tight jeans, followed by your favourite boots. Now a shirt. You dig around in the dresser searching for just the right thing. You know to look up the back for that is where you hid your old clothes when your ex had a clean out.

Do you select a t-shirt with a slogan?
(LIQUOR but I don't even know her!)
Turn to 33
Do you select a shirt with team decals?
Turn to 64

17

Cassidy, you are welcome to stay at my place to-night.'

You invite Cassidy to stay.

'But you were having a night out. I can't disrupt that.'

Cassidy seemed sincere.

'Nah it's okay. I was heading home anyway.'

You lie.

Excited about having a warm shower after days of walking, Cassidy strips quickly and leaps into the water. Out of courtesy you knock before entering the room to offer a clean towel. She giggles at your coyness.

With the water trickling down her body she invites you to join her in the shower.

'The water is lovely. You sure you don't want to join me?' You can scrub my back?'

Cassidy is tanned all over. You cannot see one strip of white skin. Compared to her you feel pale.

Splashing you with water and her giggles, Cassidy tries to lure you into the shower with her.

'You can scrub my back? Or I can scrub yours.'

It's not a tough choice. Stripping quickly you step in beside her.

Both naked, your bodies slide against each other in the small cubicle. In one smooth motion she turns you and presses your chest against the wall. Her breasts rub against your back as she lathers you up with the soap. You feel her nipples harden against your skin. Pressed close, she asks.

'Are you a dirty girl?'

Nodding is all you can do.

Using her body as a sponge, she rubs herself against you. Side to side, then up and down. Her lathered hands pull you closer. The act is so sensual that you feel like you are going to climax. Cassidy's hand slides up your inner thigh and you arch your back in response. She nibbles down your neck then returns to gnaw on your ear ever so slightly. Oh no, not the ear. It's your kryptonite. Thoughts about the club vanish from your mind.

END

18

You are disappointed that your night ended the way it did. The Swedish girls were going to leave first thing in the morning to another secluded training camp. No point in ringing them. Looking around the police station you see the detective's eyes focus on you.

You ask her out for breakfast. Surprisingly, she accepts, and you head to a local pancake house. The detective has a hilarious sense of humour and is great to talk to. As you finish your juice she asks you a question.

'Are you fully refuelled?'

'Yes. Why?'

Without a word she pays the bill, then looks you up and down.

'Want to come home with me?'

It's a bit out of the blue, but since she is the one who ruined your night, you think why not.

When you reach the detective's house, she leads you out the back where there is a private spa. Returning inside, she leaves you standing alone in thought.

Behind you are light footsteps but you think nothing of it until you feel cold metal enclose your wrists. The detective has handcuffed you. It's an odd feeling. You panic slightly.

Spinning you around the detective looks you in the eyes.

'You know what? This is going to be more fun than five Swedish girls.'

She pushes you back onto a cage you hadn't noticed. She locks you there.

'When I let you climax, keyword, let you, it will be the biggest climax you have ever had or ever will have. You hear me?'

For some reason you only have one response.

'Yes ma'am'.

The anticipation is excruciating. Looking at the detective you open your mouth.

'I said no talking.'

Scolded before any words leave your mouth, you hang in thought. While your mouth is open she pops in a small red ball.

'Ready?'

All you can do is nod or shake your head. You have no words. To the detective, it doesn't matter which you do, her mind is made up.

END

19

'I have to admit I have played with a few toys, but none as large as that one.'

You refer to the dong in the bathtub. Ginger blushes with embarrassment.

'I understand your hesitation, but understand, there is nothing wrong with toys as long as they are an extension of the passion already there.'

You hope she is not offended.

Sipping your drink, you regale to Ginger about a woman you met many years earlier.

'She actually named each toy. What's worse, is that she yelled their names when she used them.'

At the time you found this quite disturbing. Ginger agreed. You admit the woman was far more interested in the toys than in people.

Looking a little disturbed Ginger sculls her drink. You reassure her.

'If anyone chose a toy over you, Ginger, they'd be a complete idiot.'

Her sensuality was intoxicating.

'Just the thought of kissing you is sending a buzz through my body.'

You hope its not too forward of you.

She thanks you for the compliment by leaning towards you and placing her delicate lips upon yours. The kiss is better than you imagined. It was soft, full of desire. You kiss again this time with tongues. Your hand caresses her breasts as a 'sigh' escapes from Ginger's mouth. She moves her body closer to you. You embrace her fully. The kissing becomes more lustful. There is an urgent desire to remove all the obstacles between you. Most notably your clothes. Scrambling to do so, you press your flesh to hers.

Nibbling her neck, her body convulses under you as she releases another, louder sigh. Or is it a gasp? You continue in the hopes of finding out.

You spend the night appreciating each other's body. The night is one you will remember for a long time.

END

20

You think it amusing to talk to the Brazilian soccer team. Though they already have a swarm of women around them, you approach anyway. One notices you and smiles. You smile back. She greets you in broken English. Chatting to her for a while, she finds you very amusing. So much so, she invites a friend to join the conversation.

'Do you all have Brazilian wax jobs?'

You jokingly ask.

They look confused so you indicate to your crotch, pretending to wax it. Being dramatic you imitate pulling the paper strip off with a mock scream. Both laugh and respond.

'We don't understand the question, but yes, we wax here.'

They indicate their nether region.

'Hair is bad when you run. We like bare. You say its called a Brazilian? We have never heard of it referred to as that.'

'We are Brazilian!'

More laughter fills the air as they re-enact your waxing moves.

When the laughter simmers down, they become curious as to whether you play soccer. One pretends to kick a ball around then scoring while the other fake cheers. Both obviously teasing you about the waxing scenario. You admit that you have only played a few games, for fun. Nothing competitive.

'But I do work out, well occasionally.'

Not recently. Attempting to feel your muscles, they can't contain their amusement.

Another team member calls over in a language you don't understand. The two you are talking to ask if you would like to join them for a friendly game of soccer in the park across the road. Some other volunteers have been found yet they need one more.

Do you choose to play soccer in the park?
Turn to 95
Do you choose to sing karaoke instead?
Turn to 28

21

Why not a cab? It'll give you time to throw down a few more drinks before the club. Drinks are always so expensive in those places. Single life has made you more flush with cash, yet there's always that conservative gene that niggles at you.

The ride is quiet as the driver speaks poor English. You wonder why so many cab drivers are foreign, but to be honest, you don't really care. All that matters is that you get to where you want. And you're not one for forced conversation.

Up ahead, you see a woman, in a dark section of the road, trying to hail your cab. You check your watch and realise you promised to meet Maddie ten minutes ago. Surely Maddie would forgive you.

You laugh at the thought. Maddie was a womaniser, in ten minutes she would have scanned the club and made a selection. By now she was probably having 'fun' with her third one.

The street is abandoned. There are no other vehicles in sight. You have a twinge of sadness for the woman as the cab approaches the section of road where she is standing. Living around here you know how hard cabs are to get, plus most services prefer residential over street pick-ups.

You check your watch again as the cab is about to pass the woman.

Do you choose to give her a lift?
Turn to 44
Do you choose to continue onto the club?
Turn to 58

22

With one final swig of tequila, you approach Officer Goode. Taking you by surprise, she commands you to stand back and strip. Her voice is authoritative, not to mention scary, so you oblige.

'Do it slowly. I want to enjoy it.'

Her voice softened slightly.

Taking your time, you remove each item slowly. Like a striptease show you throw in a spin and butt shake here and there. Officer Goode remains where she is, but her eyes are aglow. Small beads of sweat appear on her upper lip. She licks them away slowly.

Once naked, she requests you lie on the bed. A thrill is rising within you. Officer Goode approaches. Using silk scarves she secures your wrists, then moves towards your ankles. Rolling your hands, the scarves are tighter than you expected.

Heart is thumping hard in your chest, adrenalin is seeping through your body as you squirm under her control. The silk slides easily over your last ankle, then it is tugged tight. Satisfied with the scarf's tightness, Officer Goode removes her uniform to reveal a black leather corset with matching underwear and suspenders.

You gulp as she glares at you. In a flawless motion she lifts a leather whip from the chest of drawers and slaps you across the thigh. It stings a little. A small red welt rises in the spot.

'Ow.'

You say more to yourself, raising your head to look at the spot that is stinging.

'I said no talking.'

Her scolding eyes search your body. Suddenly you realise how vulnerable you are. When you move, even a little, the scarves bite in, holding you in place. Plus, isn't there meant to be a safe word? Yes, a safe word.

'You must be punished for your violation, and I am the one to do it!'

Her voice is authoritive as she raises the whip. A perverse grin fills her face.

OMG, you so desperately want a safe word.

Turn to 93

23

It peeves you no end, that after such a lovely night, Cassidy would steal your bike. Your precious beast. Utterly bummed, you find it hard to sit and wait for the sunrise. Instead, you pack your things and start to walk down the track that brought you here. In the distance is a cloud of dust. You hope it's someone who can give you a lift, because you aren't quite dressed for hiking. Besides it's quite a distance to your house from here, and its too early to ring anyone for a lift.

The dust cloud moves closer, before you hear a familiar rumble. It's your bike! You are so excited to see Cassidy. She apologizes for scaring you.

'I'm sorry. It's just that I saw a diner as we entered the track last night. You were sleeping so peacefully, that I didn't want to disturb you. I thought I could sneak out and return before you noticed.'

In her pack she had fresh croissants and piping hot coffee.

'After such a brilliant night, I thought a romantic

breakfast on the shoreline was in order. Besides I didn't want our time together to end.'

She continued to apologise for the misunderstanding. You accept her apology and the offer to make it up to you. With toes resting in the water, you both watch the sun as it rises boldly into the sky. You wonder what the day will hold.

END

24

The suggestion takes you both by surprise. You are silently stunned and Ginger just laughs her effervescent laugh. Sadly, being so intoxicated negates any normal thinking by either of you.

'How about now?'

Suggests Ginger.

Delighted with the answer, the salesgirl openly jumps with joy before leading you to a back room where a makeshift bed happens to be. Befuddled, your mind tries to work out why a shop would have a bed in the storeroom, especially an adult shop. It takes a moment, but then... oh.

'You two get ready while I close the shop.'

Forcefully taking you by the hand, Ginger leads you to the bed. Slowly she undoes your clothing, removing each piece one by one. In your alcoholic stupor you just giggle. The giggling comes to a halt when Ginger presses her lips to yours. The kiss is magical. Next thing you know, Ginger is nibbling on your lower lip. Her teeth grip it sufficiently that you can't pull away even if you wanted to. Instead you remove Ginger's clothes, and the kissing continues.

Ginger is naked and on top of you by the time the salesgirl returns. In her hands are several demo toys. She explains each like a sales pitch, Ginger tells her not to bother explaining them, to just use them. A small giggle escapes your mouth. Turning on every single toy, the salesgirl approaches with a bemused grin. Your giggling stops and is replaced with silent wonder.

In that back room, time is lost on all of you. It isn't until you go to the drink machine for nourishment that time kicks back in. Standing naked, you look out the shop window as the sun is just peering over the horizon. Morning warmth is streaming through the glass. As you are looking out, an elderly lady walking her sausage dog happens to look in. Turning to Ginger, you speak.

'It might be time to go.'

The salesgirl agrees.

'I've got to go too. My boyfriend is being released from prison today and I need to pick him up.'

'What'd he do?'

Ginger asks out of curiosity.

'Aggravated assault.'

'Who did he assault?'

'It was somebody he caught me sleeping with. But it was just a misunderstanding, really.'

'Did you not sleep with them?'

Ginger was very invested in the answer now.

'Oh yes, I did. My boyfriend just didn't understand that we were in an open relationship. It's not his fault, he just gets jealous.'

She responded nonchalantly.

Looking at each other, you and Ginger, quickly dress to leave. Neither of you ever return to that shop again.

END

25

You love the feel of the breeze in your face and the rumble of the engine between your thighs. It's been a while since you last took the beast out for a spin. The club is a short distance away and that's a shame. Riding is just pure bliss, so you decide to veer off so as to ride a little longer. You're running late but Maddie will forgive you. The time wasn't that definite, besides you've already backed out the last two times.

As you veer around a corner you see a woman standing at the bus stop. She looks frustrated as she checks her watch. Looking at yours, you realise that there is not another bus for the night. At this time, the bus changes route and travels along the main street. The distance between here and the nightly stop is about three kilometres.

The woman's profile catches in your headlight. She is of similar age to you, and her features are quite stunning. At her feet is a knapsack with an Austrian flag on it. You make the obvious assumption, that she's a backpacker.

Do you choose to continue to the club?
Turn to 58
Do you choose to stop and give the woman a
lift?
Turn to 50

26

Talking to Kat is just odd, even so, you figure she might be well suited for a one-night stand, so you take her up on the offer. She lives in a unit just around the corner from the club. The walk is refreshing and thankfully, not much conversation is needed to get there.

Upon entering the unit Kat leaps over the couch towards a stereo, turning on some dance music. You are thankful it's loud enough to kill the need to talk. Kat, purring, seductively leads you into her bedroom, where she claws your clothes off. Still purring, she rubs against you like a cat. You think it peculiar, but with you both being naked it doesn't seem an issue. She leaps onto the bed. On all fours, she is giving you seductive eyes.

Moving closer, you grab Kat, playfully forcing her to the mattress. Above her now, with your hands upon her wrists, you hear a creak. At least you think you do. Kat, beneath you, appears not to. Her purring just grows louder. Unfazed you move to kiss her.

Suddenly there is a loud crack, a sharp pain in your head, then everything goes black. You wake up in hospital with Kat sitting next to you texting her friends. You ask what happened? She informs you that while the two of you were having fun the headboard broke away from the bed and slammed you on head.

'Fortunately I was beneath you, so I'm okay. isn't that a relief?'

'I suppose.'

Fortunate for her, not for you.

'My friends said that since you were unconscious, I should call an ambulance. Glad I did, because I couldn't move you at all.'

Looking under the covers you notice you are naked.

'Where are my clothes?'

Kat shrugs.

'Well I had to decide what to wear. Then I had to take pics for my blog. That was difficult cause you wouldn't pose right, and the lighting was wrong. Then Charlie sent me a meme about cats. It was hilarious. Do you want to see it?'

You shake your head, unable to believe her ramblings.

'No? Then the ambulance came. So you see, there was no time.'

Kat was happy with her answer. To say you were peeved was an understatement though she didn't notice and just kept rambling.

'Is it okay If I go now? My fav DJ is about to do a set at the club. Everyone's there and I'd hate to miss it.'

You wave good-bye and make a mental note to avoid people like Kat in future.

END

27

Pouring a glass of wine, you notice the bottle is empty. You don't recall drinking that much, though you do feel good. Tonight is the right occasion to wear that little cocktail dress you bought that your ex hated. Because of her, you weren't allowed to wear it yet, but tonight was the perfect opportunity. Hopefully, you had been off the market long enough that you would be classed as fresh meat. The thought thrills you.

You spend extra time in the bathroom perfecting your make-up and hair. If you're going to be fresh meat you want to be a prime piece. Sighing you think of the lost years with your ex, then grin at the thought of what she is missing out on tonight. You scull another glass of wine, from a fresh bottle, and feel it instantly boost your confidence.

The clock strikes the hour letting you know that you're running late. Even so, you return to the bathroom to ensure you look perfect. And you do.

'Cheers!'

You toast yourself, holding the glass aloft. Looking for your purse, you find it hidden in the hallway closet. Checking your watch you head to the door.

Do you choose to take a bus?
Turn to 4
Do you choose to take your car?
Turn to 73

28

Karaoke is not really your thing. Sure, your ex always wanted you to give it a go, but that's probably because she wanted to make a fool out of you. Tonight, you are feeling brave, and if nothing else you could do with an extra $500 in cash. Well, that's if you happened to win the karaoke competition. You make a song selection, hoping you know all the words.

Singing hard you try to move around the stage as if you know what you're doing. It scares you that the audience is silent. All they're doing is staring. It's quite unsettling but you continue anyway. Thinking if you are bombing miserably, just blame the alcohol.

As the song comes to its conclusion, you leap from the stage. Head bowed all you can hear is silence as the track rolls to an end. The moment is terrifying. Suddenly, the room bursts into applause and cheering. They love you. They demand more. You look up a little surprised, especially since you have only ever sung in the shower.

A staff member presents you with the cash and

asks if you would like to sing with the band who are already taking their place on stage.

Do you choose to sing with the band?
Do you choose not to sing with the band?
Turn to 43

29

You've always been rather partial to jukeboxes, so you go over to see what selection they have. Scanning the songs you hear footsteps behind you, though don't think much of it. The song you want isn't there but you keep searching in case it appears. Finally, you pick a song, as you can't stand the mix of grungy rock from the beer garden and the thump thump of the dance music. To your ears anything would be better.

As the song starts there is a voice behind you. It is familiar but one you didn't expect to hear, especially not here, not tonight. You turn to see your ex. She looks the same except her eyes look a little sadder.

'You look good.'

She states then pauses. She is probably hoping you'll return the compliment, but you don't. Looking at her feet she speaks again.

'Would you like a drink.'

You think yes, but not necessarily with her.

'Please.'

She asks. Looking in her eyes you wonder if you

can forgive her. Then again, is she actually asking for forgiveness or is she after something else. Do you care?

Do you choose to drink with your ex?
Turn to 75
Do you choose to refuse the drink with your ex?
Turn to 45

30

A couple of the soccer players exit the bus and enter the club as does the brunette. Though as she passes, the brunette gives you a sad smile. You barely notice as you laugh heartily with your new friends, Inga, Helga, Izzy, Pip and Marta.

They invite you to their hotel room which ends up being the penthouse of the local five star. You heartily accept and are soon standing with them at their door. Entering the room you are in awe. It's massive. Inga taps you on the shoulder and invites you onto the balcony. Pip is already on the phone ordering food and drinks.

From the balcony you can see the whole town. It looked amazing from up here as if you were standing amongst the stars. Helga suggests that everyone jumps into the spa. So all five girls remove their tracksuits to reveal an array of colourful bras and G-strings. They all leap in leaving you standing fully clothed and dry.

They plead with you to join them. Marta splashes you playfully, followed by Izzy and Inga. Just as you threaten revenge the doorbell rings. Room service has arrived. Helga asks you to tip the girl from a jar next to the television. Or if you prefer the girl can tip herself so that you can join them.

Do you choose to hop into the spa?
Turn to 7
Do you choose to tip the room service girl?
Turn to 32

31

As Ginger steps into the room you pretend to finish washing your hands. Apologising for taking so long, you explain rather coyly, that you were fixing your hair in the mirror.

'I'm sorry for taking so long. It's just that you are so gorgeous. To be honest I'm having trouble understanding why you invited me here. For the life of me, I can't even understand why you were at the bar alone.'

Bubbly laughter froths from her mouth. Locking eyes with you she speaks jovially.

'Obviously you were in here and up to no good. Tsk. Tsk. So stop teasing me.'

At that moment her eye catches a glimpse of something in the bath. Ginger shuffles over slowly, all the while talking to you. She's attempting to keep you distracted from what's in the bathtub.

'You are the one who is gorgeous.'

Feeling a little nervous, your hands are becoming clammy. Ginger yells before quickly clasping her hand over her mouth.

'Oh my!'

Her next words come out muffled.

'I'm so sorry.'

Ginger looks uncomfortable as she speaks.

'This is my guest bathroom, and I hardly ever come in here. Recently, my brother stayed with his boy-friend. That must be theirs. Oh, I'm so embarrassed.'

You tell her it's no big deal yet she remains apologetic. Ginger rushes you both from the bathroom and pours another drink. She gets the giggles as she whispers a question.

'Have played with toys before?'

Do you choose to answer yes?
Turn to 19
Do you choose to answer no?
Turn to 86

32

It's just plain rude not to tip hotel staff especially if you are in the penthouse. You've done it tough in jobs, knowing how hard it is to get by on minimum wage. So you walk over to the jar and look inside for the tip money. The contents take you by surprise. Sure, you expected money, but this? Looking over at the Swedish girls you slide your hand into the jar. All you can feel are rolls and rolls of cash. The Swedish girls are too preoccupied with the cans of whipped cream to notice the shocked look on your face.

You look at the room service girl who is waiting patiently. She has piercing eyes that are appealing, you smile at her and she smiles back. Your hand is still in the jar yet you can't decide what to do. Rolls of cash tumble under your fingers while you wonder how much each roll is worth. Tilting her head in a playful way, the room service girl gives you an inquisitive look.

'Are you stuck?'

'No.'

You laugh before continuing.

'Just deciding.'

Do you take a handful of cash and leave, possibly with the room service girl? Or do you just give the girl the tip and return to the five girls in the spa? These things never happen to you!

Do you choose to take some money and leave?
Turn to 94
Do you choose to tip the girl then return to the spa?
Turn to 83

33

Your hair ruffles as you slip the t-shirt on. It makes you feel good. You spray a little scent around your body, not enough to suffocate but hopefully enough to be alluring.

Heading to the kitchen you take a beer from the fridge and guzzle it down. That one's for luck. You take a second. After popping the top you drink this one a little slower.

The music is still playing. In anticipation of the night your body is pumping. You feel sixteen again, with the thrill of heading out. Taking one last look in the mirror you grab your wallet and head out the door. You stop short wondering how much you are planning to drink tonight. You check your watch again. Do you have time to wait for a cab? Extra time would allow you to drink more.

Tonight is about partying, drinking and hopefully getting laid. So what would achieve that? Alcohol or a rumbling motor bike? Admittedly you are feeling pretty awesome. The motorbike was too dangerous for

your ex. Too Dangerous! Blah, she just wasn't adventurous.

Do you choose to call a cab?
Turn to page 21
Do you choose to take your motorbike?
Turn to page 25

34

You politely decline the salesgirl's offer. Being in the shop is terrifying enough, let alone the salesgirl offering you something that looks like pesto but with no crackers.

You move around the shelves to avoid her and to find Ginger who is looking at some mechanical dildos.

'Which do you think would work better?

Ginger asks in the same manner someone would about which pasta sauce is better.

You shrug not knowing the difference. Unfortunately, the salesgirl pops up again and states that she has tried every toy in the shop, if we needed a recommendation. Both you and Ginger are shocked but attempt to look cool. While demonstrating the power of a product the salesgirl, eyeing the you both up and down, makes a statement.

'I've never slept with a woman before.'

You try to speak, nothing comes out. Ginger's eyes are wide in disbelief.

The salesgirl boldly continues.

'I definitely think it would be more fun with two women. Mainly because three is my lucky number. Do you have a lucky number?'

The only thought that hits your head is that you're lucky if you can get one woman into your bed. Plus, how does three work? All those arms and legs?

Do you choose to accept the salesgirl's offer?
Turn to 24
Do you choose to decline the salesgirl's offer?
Turn to 54

35

After another drink you both head home to relive the old times. While your ex drinks the last bottle of wine in the fridge, you drink beer. A comment is made about the uncouthness of beer but you ignore it. In the bedroom the activity is familiar and unchallenging. You have outgrown this.

Finally, you realise how much you didn't miss her. A few hours later your ex states that she is leaving you, again. Though you don't really care, you decide to put on a show and ask who this new love is. She responds snarkily.

'It's the same person I cheated on you with. Someone that truly loves me, and respects me. Someone who always puts me first. Unlike you.'

It makes you want to vomit. Your ex always put herself first. For show, you consider the idea of smashing a few plates, but think better of it. Who wants to clean up a mess? Finally, as she is leaving, she reveals her lover.

'Maddie and I are deeply in love. And there's nothing you can do about it.'

You wonder why she came up to you at the club, since they were so in love. Your ex blushes and admits that she just wanted to make sure there was nothing left between the two of you.

'Plus, I was trying to make Maddie jealous. She was chatting to some waitress.'

'Such commitment.'

You stammer before dropping another pearl of wisdom.

'So, let me get this right. You left your girlfriend alone, for the night, while she was chatting up another woman? To teach her a lesson?'

Without another word your ex slams the door and leaves your life.

Do you choose to seek revenge on Maddie?
Turn to 56
Do you choose to forget about Maddie and your ex?
Turn to 42

36

You have a strange nagging feeling about the lead singer of the band, so you approach the side of the stage. There appear to be a few groupies and you attempt to not look like one. Without looking up the singer asks if you'd like an autograph. Responding with a 'no' she looks up surprised.

Finally you recognise her, she's your dentist, Doctor Draco. Yes, that's right, you thought she was vampirish with no sense of humour. You mumble something and turn to leave yet she stops you. Taking in your features she can't quite place your face. You call her Doctor Draco and she laughs.

'My names Millie.'

Her smile is welcoming.

'So, you're not a groupie? I don't suppose you have a sore tooth then?'

You laugh and respond 'no' to both, then continue.

'I really enjoyed the show. Just wanted to let you know.'

You both stand there unsure of what to do.

'Can you sing?'

Millie asks happily.

'Only in the shower.'

You joke.

'Well then, how about joining me on stage? I'm sure the band will make us sound good.'

Do you choose to sing with the band?
Turn to 60
Do you choose to ask Millie out?
Turn to 8

37

Knowing that it is invasive to look into someone else's cabinet, you return to the lounge room. Riley is not there. You look in the kitchen. She is not there either. You hear music and decide to follow it.

As you approach the bedroom door you can see the glow of candles and the smell of fragrant oils. Your heart jumps a little. As you enter the room Riley is naked on the bed except for a few well positioned rose petals.

'I hope you don't mind.'

She pouts.

'No. Not at all.'

You respond as you remove your clothes. Her eyes light up.

'Want to join me?'

You don't have to be asked twice. As you approach the bed you lift her foot ever so gently.

'You smell nice.'

You make a sniffer dog noise around her foot then

work your way up her leg. Snuffling all the way. Riley laughs softly.

The music is soft and gentle, the same way she makes love to you. You have never felt so wanted before, and in that moment, you have never wanted anyone else as much.

Before you know it, the sun is rising. You are drained but deliriously happy. Riley offers to make breakfast for the next twenty years. You consider her proposal over scrambled eggs, French toast with a berry compote, freshly squeezed juice and crispy bacon.

END

38

With a look, you signal to the room service girl to grab a tip and leave. With attitude she says she has a tip for you.

'What?'

You answer without looking at her.

'I bet I can please you better than the five of them.'

She responds.

'Really?'

You ask questioningly. You look at the Swedish girls then look at her, doubting the possibility. The girl takes it as a challenge. She strips seductively then enters the spa. The Swedish girls are unhappy with this and start grabbing at you as if you are a prize. To be honest you really don't mind.

You ask the girls to prove who is better stating you will be an honest and fair judge. They can't decide whether to go one at a time or all at once, so you suggest they try both. You settle in for the best night of your life.

END

39

Looking through the cupboard and fridge, you realise you haven't shopped in a week. You'd like to impress Millie with your cooking skills, but they don't extend to prunes and beer. Instead, you grab the phone and call your favourite restaurant. You order a three-course banquet. Pronto!

Thankfully, Millie takes a long shower, with the delivery boy arriving well before she shuts the water off. By the time she is dry, you have the table set with your best plates and some candles to enhance the mood. Soft music is playing in the background. Millie enters the room as you are popping the cork off a nice bottle of wine you had stashed away. She smiles and comments how fancy it all looks.

'I would have been happy with toasted cheese sandwiches.'

'To be honest I ordered in. The cupboards were bare.'

Millie doesn't mind as she is starving.

'It's refreshing to have a decent shower and a

healthy meal after a show. It's been tough lately. The band has been traveling a lot. All we do is stay in cheap motels and pubs. It's getting quite depressing.'

'Well don't worry, you are always welcome to stay here.'

As an afterthought, you mention the guest bed-room.

'Don't get me wrong. I do have a guest room. I wasn't suggesting anything.'

She appreciatively smiles at you.

'Thank you. It's nice to meet someone so lovely. And decent. As the band gets better known we seem to attract a lot of weirdos. Oh, and the groupies. I'm not sure what inspires them?'

'Fame or money?'

You suggest.

'Well, whoever sleeps with me won't get either. I'm sure of that. I'm not famous, and the venues we attend barely cover a round of soft drinks.'

The two of you share a laugh.

Do you choose to make a pass at Millie?
Turn to 99
Do you choose to continue talking to Millie?
Turn to 62

40

Riley's place is a simply decorated unit, but it felt welcoming. From the windows is a wide-open view to the river. With drink in hand, you watch the lights of passing boats as the scent of a scrumptious dinner fills the air. You can't recall the last time someone cooked for you. You were always the one doing the household chores, not your ex.

Wiping your ex from your mind, you take in the view of Riley. While stirring the sauce she raises her glass to you.

'Renewed friendships.'

You smile, raise your glass and take another sip. You haven't felt this relaxed in a long time.

Dinner is incredible and the company even better. For dessert, Riley suggests you both sit on the lounge. She feeds you strawberries, one at a time. You devour them hungrily. To compliment the strawberries Riley finds a can of whipped cream in the fridge. She accidentally spills some on you and licks it up. A thrill rises within you.

Riley spills more on your breasts. She licks that up too. You are enjoying the moment but are overcome with a need to find the toilet. Too many drinks you explain. What timing.

'I promise to be back shortly. And we'll take up from here.'

You kiss her passionately before heading to the toilet. Her bathroom is quite expansive. You imagine the pair of you in the oversize tub. While washing your hands you notice the cabinet behind the mirror above the sink.

Do you choose to look in the cabinet?
Turn to 12
Do you choose not to look in the cabinet?
Turn to 37

41

You sympathize with Ginger but declare that it is a bit much to take in at the moment.

'I understand where you are coming from. I think you are very brave but I just need a moment to catch up.'

Sitting beside her, trying to find the right words, you continue.

'Look. I need to be honest with you. The male form has always repulsed me, but when I look at you I see an incredibly attractive woman. It's confusing, and I'm not sure if I am in the mindset to face that right now.'

Mixed emotions and desires flood your body. Silence fills the air as you wonder whether it would be rude to just stand and leave. As you rise, laughter bubbles from Ginger as it had at the bar. Feeling self-conscious you turn to her. She is smiling, then opens her soft lips to speak.

'You know I was only joking. I'm 100% woman.'

She smiles at your stunned look while taking your hand and placing it in her crotch.

'Come on, it was just a test to see how you react to situations. I'm a psychologist studying transsexuals.'

A noise that sounded slightly like a laugh escapes your mouth. This is doing your head in.

Ginger continues to speak.

'After all that time I spent on you, I want it repaid.'

A breathy pause has you hanging on her words.

'By double.'

Ginger's smile is wicked and alluring all at once. You are happy to oblige.

END

42

You stare at the closed door then smile to yourself. The ultimate revenge. You've known about your ex and Maddie for a while now, but you had to wait for the right opportunity.

You walk over to the dresser where you remove the film from the hidden camera. Last night, you had planned to test the couple's commitment by sleeping with one or the other. You had covered every detail, even having a dated newspaper in view of the camera. To ensure the desired result you had streamed to specially selected email addresses. Anonymously of course. The camera was set to not get your face on film. And a remote control under your pillow helped to ensure that. You heard they were getting married soon so this should test the waters a little.

Today you were starting your new life by moving overseas, you were bound to make new friends and new girlfriends. Neither your ex nor Maddie knew of your plans: just your family.

You lick the envelope which is addressed to

Maddie's ex, who is still obsessed with her. Some may call her a stalker, yet to you she is a tool for justice. A smile fills your face as you drop the envelope into a post box at the airport.

END

43

'Thanks for the amazing offer, but I can't.'

You politely turn down the offer to play with the band. The whole ordeal was quite nerve wracking, and you have an express need to visit the bathroom. A woman tries to speak to you on the way, yet you ignore her. You have no desire to wet your pants in a crowded club.

As you exit the bathroom, she approaches again. the woman just happens to be a music agent who caught your show. Strangely, she thinks you were amazing and would like to sign you to her label. You look at her in disbelief. Presenting you with a business card, you instantly recognise the business name of a global music company. You ask her if she is for real, and she states she is.

You are dumbfounded, even more so when she leads you out to an awaiting limo. She encourages you to get in first before following. Unfortunately, the agent's heel gets caught in the gutter causing her to stumble towards the door opening. Amazingly, you manage to stop her falling by pulling her on top of you. The look in her eyes is unmistakable. Your pulse is demanding. She smells amazing.

The chauffer gently closes the door before you have even released her from your grip. To be honest you don't want to release her. The weight of her body on you confirms your desire. You hope she will let you kiss her. She does. The first kiss is followed more passionately with several others.

The agent grabs at your clothes and you hers. The chauffer lowers the front screen only a fraction and asks where to? In unison you both say 'anywhere'. Neither of you care as you are too engrossed in each other.

END

44

At the very last moment, you yell at the cab driver to stop. Your conscience has overtaken any other thought. It's tough to get a cab around here especially on this dark street. The cab overshoots her by a few meters. She runs to the back door and opens it. She looks in at you.

'Sorry but thanks for stopping. I've been trying to get a cab for an hour and a half.'

Her words are breathy and sweet. She offers a smile and her hand as she enters the cab.

'Hi, I'm Cindy.'

After introducing yourself you tell the cab driver to continue to the club. You ask Cindy if that's okay because you're running late. She has no problem with it. You chat on the way. Though she is a little dishevelled her eyes are warm and welcoming. Their piercing colour, making you a little nervous.

You find out that she is a medical student from out of state. She had turned up to meet a friend. Well, a pen pal she has had since she was younger but it turned out the pen pal was a dude. A very rude one at that. She had run from his place and become terribly lost. That was why she was on the side of the road. You listen to her patiently until the cab pulls up outside of the club.

Do you choose to invite Cindy in for a drink?
Turn to 9
Do you choose to enter the club?
Turn to 58

45

You take a look at your ex and it finally hits you. How stifling she was towards you. In the relationship you weren't allowed to dress as you wanted, work at the job you wanted or even buy something for the house because it didn't go with her plan. The realization of this makes you feel stronger inside.

'I wouldn't lower myself to your level. To be honest, whoever you left me for, deserves you. They did me a favour. In a way I pity them, having to live with your controlling antics.'

These comments infuriate your ex who is now standing and making a scene. You wave the bouncer away.

'Are you done?'

You ask sarcastically.

She turns to leave but turns back and speaks. There is venom in her words.

'I left you for Maddie.'

With the sentence complete she walks away from you and up to Maddie at the bar where she passionately kisses her. The waitress with whom Maddie was talking, leaves in disgust. Maddie casts a worried look towards you but you pretend not to see them. They hurry out of the door.

Do you choose to seek revenge on Maddie?
Turn to 56
Do you choose to enter the dance club?
Turn to 3
Do you choose to enter the beer garden?
Turn to 61

46

The option of ingredients, though limited, does not restrict you in coming up with a fun meal of only finger foods. Clearing the furniture in the lounge, you set up a blanket for an indoor picnic. Millie enters just as you are lighting the candles.

She looks seductive in one of your t-shirts and cartoon boxers.

'I hope you don't mind. I accidentally left my change of clothes in the band's van.'

'No problem at all. You look amazing.'

Sitting on the blanket Millie admires the selection of tiny foods. You serve her by placing small titbits on her tongue. Quickly eating each piece, her tongue begs for more. Every now and then she nips you playfully.

She places a cream dipped strawberry in your mouth. Her fingers are rough, and some cream is left on your lip. Millie leans forward and kisses it away. Next, she dabs cream on your nose then kisses it. You attempt to do the same to her, but you end up in a food fight. Cream is everywhere and before you know it, she has you pinned to the floor. She speaks in a husky murmur.

'Forfeit or suffer the consequences.'

You are so curious about the consequences that you struggle slightly. From that action, she responds by licking the food from your body. You commit to never forfeiting again.

END

47

As both you and Ginger are so intoxicated, you happily follow the salesgirl into the change room. You look at the green stuff in the pot and wonder where the crackers are, for it looks like pesto. The salesgirl gives you some direction.

'Put some on your finger and rub it on your clit.'

Ginger looks at you and giggles, yet she is the first to try it.

'Mmm.'

Is Ginger's only response. The salesgirl is looking at you hopefully, so you scoop up a blob and do the same.

'Can you feel it going hot then cool?'

The salesgirl asks excitedly.

Ginger practically screams yes but all you can feel is an intense heat. So intense it feels as if it is burning through your body. You squeal and ask for the bathroom. The salesgirl says there is none, but she has a bottle of cold soft drink behind the counter.

You run to the counter and snatch up the soft

drink. Pouring it down your pants you are feeling soothed until you realise everyone in the shop is looking at you. Ginger, trying to smother her amusement, drops a few toys on the counter.

'I'll take these.'

After paying the salesgirl, Ginger takes you by the hand and leads you back to her place. Smiling, she says.

'I'll look after your boo boo.'

END

48

The officer seems approachable though she is not smiling. Trying your best line, you attempt an innocent smile. Bending through the window to get a closer look, she nods then returns to a standing position. Her hand starts writing on her fine book.

'I'm sorry officer.'

You try and snatch a glimpse of her name badge. The name reads S.M. Goode. You wonder what the S and M stand for but decide not to ask.

'Officer Goode. I have no excuse except I was running late to meet a friend at the club. Just down the road.'

Her eyes lift momentarily from the paper she is writing on.

'A romantic friend?'

'N-n-no.'

Is all you manage to stutter. Authoritive figures always make you nervous. Officer Goode tears the paper from the book. Carefully folds it, precisely creasing each fold. Just when you think she is about to hand you the ticket she places the paper between her breasts. In total awe, she presses her breasts through the car window. Her buckle is scratching the door but you hardly notice.

Do you take the paper with your hand?
Turn to 66
Do you take the paper with your mouth?
Turn to 100

49

In the far corner of the bar you remain. Every now and then, Jackie brings you a refill. You know not to hit on her as her girlfriend is the bouncer of the dance club, and you love to dance. The room isn't jumping as much as you would have liked. The beer garden is noisy especially when some soccer girls turn up.

Suddenly, from behind you, two girls burst out of the bathroom arguing loudly. As you turn to look, one grabs the other's hair. Fists start to fly as does the hair pulling and swearing. You look around but no one else notices. Jackie is away from the bar and there is no other staff member in sight.

The fight is quite amusing though it looks rather vicious. You step forward to break it up but neither girl listens. You flash your detectives' badge but that doesn't work either. A fist flies loose and collects you on the right cheek. That's going to bruise. Finally, you draw your gun and that gets the girls' attention.

They have some feeble excuse for arguing. You scold them about endangering others.

Do you choose to take them to the police
station?

Turn to 14

Do you choose to let them off with a warning?

Turn to 67

50

You pull up next to the woman, who introduces herself as Cassidy, a backpacker from Austria. It takes a few minutes, but you explain how the buses run differently at this time. She curses herself for being so dumb. Laughing at her accent you offer her a lift.

Cassidy smiles at you and explains the awful day she's had. She had hoped to see something interesting but for the last four days, she'd seen nothing but the inside of buses. Cassidy explains, that she is a country girl who is feeling claustrophobic in this town. You agree that it does get a bit suffocating.

Not far from town is a lake surrounded by open country and forest. You describe its beauty to Cassidy who sadly responds that if the buses don't go there, or near it she wouldn't be able to make it, though it does sounds amazing. Sighing, she says that she misses the stars. You love the stars too. Looking up past the streetlight glare, you realise how much the house lights blur out their sparkling beauty. Memories of wishing upon stars as a child floods your mind.

Do you choose to take Cassidy to the bus stop?
Turn to 97
Do you choose to take Cassidy to the lake?
Turn to 89

51

Ginger's house is rather impressive. Cool leather couches, plenty of chrome and glass. Decorated with plenty of artifacts from around the world. It's in a style that makes you think a gay man designed it. She offers you a glass of wine and a platter of cheese, that seemingly appears from nowhere. You happily accept as she joins you on the lounge.

The conversation covers a range of topics. Ginger is an entertainer who is well travelled. You feel slightly insecure in her company so you excuse yourself to the bathroom. You quickly phone Maddie who tells you to go for it and stop doubting yourself. Washing your hands you look at yourself in the mirror.

Admittedly you are attractive, so Ginger shouldn't be out of your league. Besides, she approached you, so what does that say? Hopefully that she finds you desirable.

You try and rub a mark from your face that you see reflected but it is a mark on the mirror. You wipe it gently and the mirror pops away from the wall. It is a mirror cabinet. You look around, though you know the door is locked behind you.

Do you choose to shut the cabinet?
Turn to 10
Do you choose to look in the cabinet?
Turn to 74

52

The address on the paper appears to be for an abandoned motel. Looking about the empty carpark, you are about to leave, when you see Officer Goode's bike parked outside a room towards the back. The light is on. You park and approach the door. Before you can knock a voice calls out.

'What took you so long?'

Without a word you enter to see Officer Goode still in uniform. She shuts the door behind you.

'Drink?'

She sets two shot glasses out next to a bottle of tequila. You glance around the room. It looks like any other motel room except for the large metal army chest on the floor. Officer Goode sees you staring at it.

'So you want to get straight to it, do you?'

You look bewildered until she opens the metal chest which is jam packed with every kind of sex toy imaginable. You grab the bottle of tequila and scull a portion. Looking at the chest again, you take another swig.

Officer Goode looks you up and down, like you were a piece of meat at the butchers.

'Yes, you'll do. You'll do just fine.'

Do you choose to leave?
Turn to 84
Do you choose to stay?
Turn to 22

53

With a seductive smile Ginger breathlessly says she is a taker, though you will have to catch her first. She runs from the bathroom with you in hot pursuit. Seductively stripping clothes from her lush body as she runs around the dining room. Ginger throws clothing in your path.

'How much do you want me?'

She teases before heading towards the lounge room.

You are panting, more with excitement than with exhaustion. Ginger is close to naked. Moonlight from the window, glimmers off her skin, showing you how beautiful she truly is. You are throbbing. The dong bouncing in your hand. You want her now, so you leap over the lounge to reach her.

You miscalculate the height required for your jump, and your foot catches. This off balances you and you fall heavily. Yet you have so much forward momentum that you bounce off the lounge and onto the glass coffee table. It smashes beneath you. As glass flies everywhere, the dong, which you unknowingly threw into the air, smacks you in the head knocking you unconscious.

You wake about an hour later, completely naked. Ginger enters the room, dong in hand.

'Let's play it safe. How about you be the taker?'

END

54

It's a relief when Ginger politely refuses the sales-girl's offer. Making a hasty selection, you place it on the sales counter. Ginger's selection joins yours. The salesgirl looks a little sad when the two of you wish her a good night and leave.

You both can't believe what happened. Laughing all the way home, the two of you finally stumble through Ginger's front door. Ginger makes a suggestion.

'How about another drink?'

You counter.

'Surely we have had enough?'

She responds with confidence.

'For courage!'

Laughing, you tear the new toys from the packets. Unfortunately, you both forgot to purchase batteries. As all the local shops are closed, you check any available remote controls. Unfortunately, they have the wrong size batteries. As the salesgirl might mistake it for a change of mind, in regards to her offer, neither of you dare return to the adult shop for batteries. The situation seems overwhelmingly humorous.

Instead, Ginger and you lie on the bed laughing hysterically. Sleep overtakes you both, and the room falls silent. You wake to a rising sun and the chirp of birds. Last night was immensely fun. Ginger rolls over and smiles at you.

'So, you want to do it the old fashion way?'

Laughter fills the room once again.

END

55

The cute girl on the dance floor is happy when you approach. You lean in and whisper your name in her ear. She smiles and returns the favour.

'Kat. You can call me Kitty Kat, purrrrrrr.'

'Nice to meet you Kat. Can I buy you a drink?'

She nods before you lead her to the bar. Conversation with Kat is limited. All she seems to do is giggle, play with her nails and send text messages. You get frustrated and let the music take the place of words. You scan the room. It's busy and hectic as a good dance club should be. The music is calling, so after finishing your drink you ask Kat if she wants to dance once again.

Returning to the dance floor Kat dirty dances against you. Others watch her move seductively around. You feel like she's rubbing on you like a cat, but enjoy the attention anyway as it stirs something inside of you. Moving up your body Kat's mouth whispers in your ear.

'Take me home now, purrrrrr.'

You lean back slightly taking in her face. Things were happening way quicker than you ever thought possible. You wonder if that is a good thing?

Do you choose to accept Kat's offer?
Turn to 26
Do you choose to decline Kat's offer?
Turn to 76

56

Though you're not a stalker, you always pondered what you would do to someone who cheated on you. To be honest your ex was never worth the effort. In fact, you know you are better off without her. Maddie, on the other hand, was someone you thought you could trust. Since you can't, you get straight into action.

You collect as many garden gnomes as you can, big laughing ones, naked ones, ones with shovels and ones without. You aim to secretly insert them in the most inconvenient places in Maddie's life.

The first one is left standing at her door holding a sign saying *'I know what you did.'* You also plant a picket line of gnomes along her front path. Each one holding similar signs with accusations.

Yet the task doesn't finish there. You sit one in the passenger seat of her locked car just waiting to go for a drive. When she gets to work there is one waiting on her office chair. You amaze yourself by how creative you have become, planting gnomes all around town waiting for her. At her favourite restaurant. At the hairdressers. Even at the dentist, waiting in the chair next to her. The proudest moment is the one you slipped into her bed while she slept.

Maddie has a near break down. Gnomes are taking over her life. By the time she comes to see you, you've lost interest in the whole thing, so you wish her luck with your ex.

'And I never want to see either of you again.'

Feeling happy with the outcome, you also discover that the girl at the nursery, where you buy your gnomes, has become quite infatuated with you. When you invite her to dinner, she brings you an exclusive, one-off, gnome that she handmade herself. It has an uncanny likeness to you.

END

57

There's no way you aren't going to let a little pain stop you from partying. With the quantity of drinks people have bought you, you feel numb to any pain. The band has returned to the stage and is playing as hard as ever. The Brazilians are the centre of the party and the room is nearly to capacity.

You remain seated because you are having trouble walking. A woman, who watched the game, notices your discomfort and approaches.

'You okay?'

She asks indicating to your leg.

You tell her what happened.

'It's become numb now due to the alcohol.'

'Hey, I'm a doctor. Would you like me to take a look?'

You respond in your drunken haze without much thought.

'I love playing doctors. Sure you can examine me.'

In response to your rudeness, she squeezes your leg making you yell in pain.

'Well, it's not broken then.'

She laughs stating that only the hard-core types can play doctor. You feel scolded.

'It is slightly dislocated. I'd be happy to set it back if you can handle the pain?'

'Sure. I've got a high pain threshold.'

Gritting your teeth, and clenching the bar, you allow her to set it back while pretending it's not painful. In reality you have never felt anything like this before.

'If you really do like pain, I know another club around the corner that may be more, well, suitable?'

You politely refuse even though she is giving you inviting eyes, and sliding her hand up your inner thigh.

'As much as I'd love that, tonight isn't good for me. How about another night?'

In truth the mix of pain and alcohol has made you incredibly nauseous. You excuse yourself and head to the toilet where you promptly throw up. Washing your pale face in the mirror, you know it's time to head home.

Next time you are watching women's soccer, you regale the story to your friends how you scored against the Brazilian goalie. Only a few facts are ignored in the process.

END

58

You are happy to have finally made it to the club. The whole place is full of life and action. The beer garden is a mess of tangled bodies as they dance to the live band. The grungy rock sound is punctuated with loud cheering.

In the main bar there are plenty of people chatting. Looking around you see the jukebox has fallen quiet. Over at the bar you see Maddie talking to a waitress who is short but well endowed. Maddie holds up the one minute finger, but knowing her, it could also mean I'll catch up with you another night as I have a live one on the hook.

While you're waiting you peak into the dance club and see another tangle of bodies all hot and sweaty. The beat is rapid as the DJ loads another disc. Scanning the crowd the DJ selects a different tone dial. The music changeover is rapid allowing the dance flow to continue.

Looking around you wonder where to go first. It all looks so inviting, and all the options have potential.

Do you choose to enter the dance club?
Turn to 3
Do you choose to put a song on the jukebox?
Turn to 29
Do you choose to interrupt Maddie?
Turn to 85
Do you choose to enter the beer garden?
Turn to 61

59

You accept the detective's apology, then request to make a phone call. You call the hotel to see if the Swedish girls are still there. They are, so the hotel puts you through.

A familiar voice answers the phone. It is Maddie. Apparently she met two soccer players at the club and they invited her back to their room. When she got there, she found five, terribly sad but terribly horny, soccer players in the spa.

So the eight of them spent a wild night drinking, eating and having sex. You are happy for your friend but imagine how that could have easily have been you.

'How'd you find me?'

You make up some idiotic excuse.

'Hey, the girls have left for some secluded training for another two weeks. I'm here alone and don't have to leave till check out time.'

Maybe the night isn't fully lost.

'What? You need company?'

You hope the dejection doesn't show in your voice. Remember: that could have been you!

'Nah. Can you pick me up? I forget where my car is.'

How selfish you think, but you agree anyway.

'I suppose. Just let me detour home first.'

'All good. I'm getting a free massage at the hotel at the moment.'

You pick Maddie up as agreed. All the way home she tells you about the awesome night she had. Then she tells you about the fool who left the girls alone in the spa.

'Can you believe that? Abandoning hot chicks in a spa? And they were as horny as hell.'

There's only one way for you to respond without looking like a complete idiot.

'No. I can't believe it.'

The rest of the drive was a bit of a blur.

END

60

Even though you've never sung, other than in the shower, you were happy to dive on stage with Millie. She proposed a duet and the crowd cheered. Feeling a little nervous, the band starts playing. The song isn't that familiar, Millie is singing the main part, so you leap off an amp in an attempt to make your performance more dramatic. The crowd loves it.

You get right into it, forgetting about Millie. You leap around like a mad woman, and the audience goes berserk. You sing with all your heart. As a grand finale you surf the crowd. As the music stops, the crowd place you back on stage, and demand more. You take a bow as Millie snatches the microphone from you.

She signals to a bouncer who forcibly removes you from the stage. The audience boo's to no avail. Announcing your night is over, the bouncer throws you out the door. The bass player follows.

'That was the best performance the band has ever done. Can I get your number? We've been dying to find a replacement for Millie. You are perfect! Mind if I contact you, once we kick her out?'

It takes the band several months to get rid of Millie, but only twenty-four hours for the bass player to call you for a date.

END

61

The beer garden is the place for you. The live band is rocking and an appreciative crowd is screaming. You enter the area and hit the bar first. With drink in hand you watch the lead singer jump around stage. She looks strangely familiar but you can't quite place her.

Looking around there is a sea of faces. In the far corner is a sports team of some sort. You overhear a couple of girls saying they are the Brazilian women's soccer team. From where you are standing they look pretty wild.

As you are deciding what to do, the band call for a break. You are sure you know the lead singer. One of the bar staff jump up on stage and declares a karaoke moment. The winner will get to sing a song with the band and receive $500. It sounds tempting. You watch the first contestant jump up on stage. Their voice is hitting notes only an injured wild animal would know. Add to that their less than co-ordinated body and you know, they aren't going to win. They bomb dramatically but the drunks in the room cheer anyway. You are embarrassed for them.

The next contestant is much better though not perfect. Her movements are more fluid, suiting the song she is singing. Surprisingly, she gets even less cheers from the drunks. It's probably because she didn't wet her t-shirt before jumping on stage, like the first contestant. You wonder if you should enter the competition.

Do you choose to talk to the Brazilian soccer team?
Turn to 20
Do you choose to enter the karaoke competition?
Turn to 28
Do you choose to talk to the lead singer of the band?
Turn to 36

62

Looking at her dimpled cheeks, and how passion-ately she speaks about singing, you feel wrong in wanting to hit on her. You allow her to ramble, all the while admiring her changing eyes, the way she bites her lower lip when she's unsure of something and the way her nose twitches when she's mad.

In a matter of hours you feel every one of those actions imbedded into your life. You can't imagine living without them. Suddenly she apologizes for hog-ging all the talk and asks about you. For the first time in your life you reveal your dream to someone. You have a desire to be a writer. Millie is so easy to talk to and she accepts your dream. She encourages you to pursue it. Jumping up she runs to the door to grab her acoustic guitar. Pulling it from the case she drags you to the lounge. Her excitement is contagious. She needs some new songs for their upcoming album and asks you to write the lyrics. Initially you protest but when she plays the music you feel it rush through your body thrusting inspiration to the top.

The whole next day, the two of you are consumed with music and lyrics. Without knowing it, you discover a whole new career. Millie's band becomes an international success within six months because of a song you and she wrote that night. As a song writing team, you create many number one hits for an array of artists. You treasure that night with Millie immensely, but not as much as the intimate relationship you develop with her. You are overjoyed to find your true soul mate. Someone who helps you to grow.

END

63

You think it wise to seek medical attention as the pain is near unbearable. You manage to get from the club to the emergency room of the local hospital. There is quite a line and since you are not bleeding they do not class you as in need of urgent care. Asking for pain killers, the nurses' joke that you have had enough alcohol for the night and it might be best to sit on that for a while. You are not impressed but have little choice.

The night has been long and you are nearly asleep when they finally call your name. The nurse asks you to lie on a bed in an isolated room to wait for the doctor. Life fills your body when you see the doctor. She is tall with auburn hair, her lips are heart shaped. A warm smile fills her face as she greets you. You regale the story of how you hurt your leg. She is a big fan of soccer and is amazed that you could score against such a fantastic goalie. Her eyes show that she is impressed, even with you downplaying the event. The doctor makes a bigger fuss of you.

She sends you to x-ray and is in the room on your return. Unfortunately, your leg is broken so it will need to be plastered. She continues to talk with you as it sets. Conversation with her is light and easy. You enjoy it immensely. When you are discharged, she wraps her arm around your shoulder as she helps you with your crutches to the door. Her sweet scent over-whelms you. Turning to go back into the hospital she stops. Hurriedly she takes a pen from her pocket and writes a number on your stark white cast.

'Call me.'

She yells as she vanishes into the hospital.

END

64

Before you put on the shirt, you decide it's time for a beer. The six pack had been chilling all day in anticipation. When you swing open the fridge you see a bottle of wine, your ex's favourite. You cringe at the thought of all the wine you've had to drink since being with her. Beer was always your favourite, and the basic ones at that, yet she would only let you drink fancy imported beers. They always tasted odd.

You realise how much of a puppet you were and vow not to be that again. Referring to your ex as 'ventrilobitch', a reference to you being a puppet and her the evil ventriloquist, you swig the first beer. The cold liquid rushes down your throat as if it was your first drink after being lost in a desert. The second you appreciate more by sipping it slowly.

Buttoning up your shirt you realise that you have lost a little weight. You flex your muscles and think that the women will have trouble resisting you. Well at least you hope they will. The clock strikes the hour and you check your watch to confirm. You're running a little later than you thought but you still stop at the fridge to grab another beer.

You look around for your wallet before checking the clock again.

Do you choose to take a bus?
Turn to 4
Do you choose to take your motorbike?
Turn to 25

65

Quickly grabbing the dong as the door slides open, you toss up whether to remain standing or to jump in the bath. Though the dong is heavier than you expect. Holding it with two hands, you hope it will stop wobbling around so much.

Ginger steps through the door, and sees you holding the dong. Her face is a mix of surprise and excitement.

Embarrassed by the situation, you hide your discomfort with the first random question that comes to mind. It's randomness even surprises you.

'Are you a giver or a taker?'

Does she respond as a giver?
Turn to 6
Does she respond as a taker?
Turn to 53

66

Taking the piece of paper with your hand, you thank the officer. For some reason, she looks at you in disgust. Before she turns to leave, she snatches the paper and eats it in front of you.

A cloud of confusion encases you as she rides off on her bike. It screeches around the corner as you re-alise you didn't get fined. You shrug and wonder why.

Checking your watch you are now late and are even keener to get to the club. You're hoping it will be a good night and that you may get lucky.

Though the situation with the police officer was odd, you think nothing of it till a news report later in the week. It's about a female police officer who had been dismissed for sexually punishing red light offenders. You curse yourself for failing to be a victim.

Turn to 58

67

The girls weren't hurting anyone, other than them-
selves, so you give them a warning and let them go.
Jackie returns in time to see you getting slugged. She
offers you a bag of ice as you sit at the bar, feeling
sorry for yourself.

A woman approaches and sits next to you.

'You okay?'

Her name is Pip and she's a doctor.

'Mind if I look at your cheek?'

Turning your face slightly, she gently places her
palms on either side of your chin. Pip's fingers gently
press around the struck area. Wincing a little, you try
to act brave even though it hurts like hell.

'You may have a broken cheek bone.'

She presses it again before kissing the spot.

'No, you're fine.'

Pip winks at you but fails to let your face go.
Gazing into each other's eyes, she kisses you gently
on the lips.

'You taste mighty fine too.'

You laugh at her boldness. Pip asks if you'd like to go back to her place and play doctors, nurses or police officer. Whichever you prefer. You take her up on the offer and head back to her place for an interesting night of role-playing.

END

68

Looking at the drunks, you surmise it would be wiser to do something charitable, so you offer to assist Lucy. She's very pleased. Surprisingly, the shelter is only another two stops away. You have lived in this town a long time but never knew it was there.

The people at the shelter are welcoming. Like Lucy, you put on a kitchen apron and start prepping vegetables. You need instruction as your cooking skills are very basic. At home you just prefer to microwave a complete meal or order in. This is a whole new experience.

Serving the food is nearly as much fun. For the whole night Lucy hasn't left your side. The two of you have been joking and laughing. At one point Lucy even whispers in your ear.

'You are incredibly cute.'

You are unsure whether the reference was in a sexual way or a funny way. It doesn't matter, you are having fun.

Even washing up doesn't seem much of a chore,

with Lucy to joke with. By the time it is all done, you feel a little tired. Lucy asks if you would like to join her for a late movie, as a way of thanks for helping.

Do you choose to go to the movie?
Turn to 82
Do you choose to go home?
Turn to 13

69

My, my, aren't you a naughty little thing. You definitely enjoy exploring your limits, sexual or otherwise. Though no page has led to this one, you have found it! Congratulations. Obviously, the excitement you feel is beyond measure. And rightly so.

Unfortunately, you do not make it to getting dressed for your big night out. While standing naked in front of the mirror an eerie green glow comes through the window. Though you know you should be scared, you aren't. A momentary flash blinds you. When you open your eyes everything is hazy, like in a dream. Rapidly squeezing your eyes you hope the picture clears. And it does.

In front of you stand two female warriors, dressed in skimpy leather outfits. Both are tall, tanned and very muscular. They remind you of female versions of Tarzan. A book you loved as a child. Though your surroundings definitely aren't a jungle.

You are standing in what feels, and looks, like a space ship. There are stars beyond the circular windows. Odd controls with flashing buttons and levers are against one wall. Beyond them are some seats. The two primitively dressed warriors, with swords on their waist, look out of place with such a background. For some odd reason you have forgotten that you are naked.

'Where am I? Is this a UFO?'

The taller of the two laughs before she approaches you with a robe.

'No. Aliens don't really exist. We are Amazonian warriors and our technology is beyond basic comprehension. If we desire we can travel faster than light. Or, Alternatively, go back in time. We have many other skills too but you will just have to wait to understand them.'

You look a little confused. Not confused enough to reject the robe. You put that on hastily, yet find a moment to admire its softness. The warriors apologise for the roughness of snatching you from your life.

'We use the green light method for abducting people so that our technologies are not discovered. People assume its aliens, and since so many people don't believe they exist, abductees aren't always listened to. It provides a cloud of doubt.'

The second warrior steps forward.

'It provides secrecy for us to go about our business. Besides that, it is the easiest way for us to collect breeding stock.'

You recall the stories you have heard about alien

abduction, and consider it's relationship to breeding stock. All you have at hand is a smart arse comment.

'Anal probing really has nothing to do with breeding, as far as I'm concerned!'

The two warriors nod in agreement and offer a smile.

'We whole-heartedly agree. Though one of our scientists believes its the best way to get to the truth about someone.'

Here the two warriors look at each other and the first speaks again.

'Honestly, I think they may be a little perverted.'

Continue to 72

70

You accept Cindy's offer, as she seems rather nice. It doesn't hurt that she is good looking. The cab continues around the corner to a large motel chain. Out of courtesy you pay the fare before going to Cindy's room.

She invites you to take a seat on the bed while she slips into something more comfortable. You are obliging to no end. As you sit there she tells you to get a drink. There is a bottle of scotch on the small writing table. Not your favourite drink, but you have it anyway. On top of what you've already had, it makes you warm and tingly inside.

Cindy enters the room in a lacy French maids outfit. You feel your body surge in excitement. She acts a little coy as she helps you to strip. Her kisses are warm and wet. The same as you are feeling. You squeeze her arse and you both laugh.

'Would it be okay if I tie you to the bed?'

Cindy asks in a coy manner which gives you a sense of mutual trust.

'I don't see why not.'

Cindy produces some ribbon from under one of the pillows. Initially she tickles your body with them before securing each limb to the bed. Her nipples brush across your mouth as she tightens your right hand.

'Secure?'

She asks.

You smile and test the ribbons.

'Yes.'

Her head is thrown back in a laugh. You are turned on even more. She approaches and places a kiss on your lips.

'Thanks babe.'

Continue to 71

71

'For what?'

You ask, as she dresses slowly, then proceeds to empty your wallet before walking out the door. She comes back momentarily just to collect the scotch.

Initially you think she is playing with you, but then she doesn't return. You struggle most of the night to untie yourself. When you finally do, you shower and get dressed. It is nearly dawn as you surmise that she probably hasn't paid for the room. With no money and no car there is little you can do.

You slip out of the room hoping the motel manager doesn't see you. The walk to your house is some distance so you ring Maddie. She sounds like she is still partying and barely noticed you didn't turned up last night.

You feed Maddie a line about seducing a tourist and spending a wild night with her. Explaining that you were so drunk, you accidentally spent every cent. She's just leaving the club so she organizes for her cab to swing by and pick you up.

In the cab are three bikini models who are very pleased to meet you. Maddie declares the party is moving to her house so you join them. At least the outing wasn't a total bust. Worth every cent actually.

END

72

'You must note that the returned abductees are not perfect specimens. Their physicality is lacking, their mental awareness falls short and their appearance is, well, not the elite of their kind.'

Speaks the second warrior in a serious tone.

This makes you laugh and the warriors laugh with you. You raise your concern about being breeding stock.

'It is not really what I had in mind for my life.'

'Do not fear, you are far from breeding stock.'

You feel a little relieved until you remember the anal probing. Subconsciously your hands move to cover your arse. The warrior continues to speak not noticing your action.

'A long time ago one of our breeders managed to escape. With her she took a child. That child had carefully been bred. Its genes are faultless. Our scientists had created the perfect woman – a fitness second to none; a mind that was brilliant yet still maintained common sense; and a look that was breathtaking in any culture. That child was to become our next queen.'

You make a comment about wishing to meet such a woman. At this the warriors bow their heads.

'You are our long lost queen. We have come to return you to your rightful place. Every Amazonian woman worships you. There is nothing that a single one of us would not do for you.'

You are completely stunned but realise there are moments in life when you just have to accept your fate

'How long till we get home then?'

'The journey is as long as you wish it to be. Until you decide, we have been selected as your sexual slaves, no request is beyond us.'

As they finish speaking you realise you are on an incredibly large bed and both warriors are joining you.

END

73

Jumping into your car, you rev the engine. When your ex left, you took some of your house savings and bought your dream car. A convertible. It was fast and hot, just like you. Well at least you hoped you both were. As the fresh night air brushes through your hair a howl of delight escapes your lips

Looking about, you survey the town. Not much is happening except a cab picking up a woman, on a dark part of the road. She is rather cute, shame the cab beat you to her otherwise you might have offered her a lift. The club isn't far so you're only ten minutes late. Surely Maddie won't be upset.

You laugh at the thought. You know you're running a little late but Maddie definitely will forgive you. The time wasn't that definite, besides she knows you've backed out the last two times.

The night is going to be great no matter what. You are primed and feeling good thanks to the few drinks you've already had. You look around at the empty streets and think how boring this suburb is. Nothing ever really happens here.

Up ahead the lights turn orange. You know they will be red before you hit the line.

Do you choose to run the red light?
Turn to 5
Do you choose to stop at the light?
Turn to 81

74

Knowing it's an invasion of privacy, you still choose to look into the cabinet. Curiosity always gets the better of you. What you see takes you by surprise. Inside the cupboard are only a few things. A hairbrush, a toothbrush, some toothpaste, an incredibly large tub of personal lubricant and the largest dong you have ever seen.

The last two items leave you a little flabbergasted. Admittedly, it also leaves you a little curious. Your thoughts drift to Ginger and the possibilities the toys may offer. They're in her house. They were easy to find. Maybe she uses them to hint at something?

A rattle on the door disrupts your thoughts. It's Ginger. Just as you try to shut the cabinet door quietly the dong drops to the floor. The bathroom door is now being unlocked from the other side. Quickly shutting the cabinet, you scan the floor and find the dong has bounced into the bath.

As you yell the word 'coming', Ginger begins to

slide the door open. A decision needs to be made. And quickly.

Do you choose to leave the dong in the bath?
Turn to 31
Do you choose to pick up the dong?
Turn to 65

75

Your ex looks so sad, and pathetic, but you decide to have a drink with her. Deep down, you know it's probably not the best choice, especially when you see the expression on Maddie's face. The only reason, you can justify to yourself, is that you had shared five years together. Surely, that meant something?

Sitting at a booth, conversation is initially awkward, then it steers to the good times. The shared memories with a person is one of the things you missed most. Yes, new memories, with someone new could be made, but there is something reassuring about sharing common stories. Was that bad? About an hour later your ex reaches across the table and puts her hand on yours.

'I'm sorry. What I did was wrong. I hurt you. Hurt you badly. For that I'm sorry.'

Her eyes seem sincere. She was always able to work around you, but deep down you really didn't mind. You loved her. She looks into your eyes.

'Can I go home with you? I miss the smell of you. The feel of you.'

Do you choose to take your ex, home?
Turn to 35
Do you choose to reject your ex's request?
Turn to 45

76

Though Kat was looking seductive, you realise that dead conversation meant dead in bed, sexually. It could well be a coyote ugly moment if you went home with her. You'd definitely want to gnaw your arm off in the morning if you woke up beside that. While Kat spun, at a dizzying pace, you dance backwards out of her range. Soon enough there is a crowd of people between you.

Turning towards the bar you see a woman sitting alone. You think she's worth hitting on.

'Buy you a drink?'

She accepts with a nod. You attempt to start a conversation but the woman says nothing. All she does is smile at you while her eyes check you out: from head to toe. To your surprise, she grabs you by the wrist and leads you to the toilets.

Thrusting you into a stall the woman ravages you with kisses. One hand locks the door while her other removes your underwear. It feels a bit rushed till you feel her mouth upon you and you let out a moan.

Attempting to muffle it another replaces it. A knock on the stall disturbs your pleasure. You manage to stutter out the word 'busy'. Thankfully the person leaves.

The woman continues to delight you until you feel that you can no longer stand. Eventually, to your disappointment, she stops. Placing one last kiss on you, she leaves the stall. You lock the door behind her and sit for a while. By the time you recoup enough energy to enter the dance club, the woman is no longer in sight. With renewed vigour, you dance till three a.m., then go home alone but satisfied.

END

77

You have no phone, no bike, so there is little you can do. Other than walking out of there. Figuring that it is such a nice day, you might as well spend it lazing by the lake. Lying on the waters edge, you feel the water ripples tickling your toes. From out of nowhere, you hear an engine, a bit like a dirt bike but it's coming from the water.

You look up and see a jet ski approaching. The woman stops the craft near you.

'Do you know much about engines?'

'A little. Want me to help?'

After a quick look you discover it's a loose spark plug lead. Within a minute, it is reconnected and the jet ski is purring as it should.

'Wow, you're amazing. How about I buy you a breakfast as thanks? There's a diner on the far side of the lake.'

You happily accept, as your tummy is rumbling loudly.

The lake is brilliant with the morning sun sparkling

off the ripples. Mischka, your saviour, pulls the jet ski up to a small jetty which joins the diner. Just as you enter, you see your bike parked in the car park. Looking around, you see Cassidy scoffing down some bacon and eggs. You walk over and snatch your keys, wallet and mobile phone. This takes her completely by surprise and she nearly chokes on the food.

You ignore the chocking and head back to the table containing Mischka, happy to have your bike back. Like nothing has happened you order breakfast and spend a glorious morning with Mischka, who is ever so excited to go on the back of your motorbike.

END

78

Ginger is sobbing as she looks at you. You are pacing around the room trying to make sense of it all. As Ginger explains that she didn't mean for a physical relationship to start until you had gotten to know each other better, you sit beside her. She sobs louder so you wrap her in your arms.

You shush her like a baby and explain how the situation has taken you by surprise.

'I'm sorry for my reaction.'

You apologise for your response and ask her to understand where you are coming from. The sobbing slows.

'You are very brave for making such a big life decision. I respect you for it. Not many people can take such a bold step.'

Her face brightens. Ginger looks at you, so you cup her face in your hands, and kiss her. The kiss is amazing and you wish to voice how you feel. Words flood your mind. You are unsure if they are right or wrong, but they are all you have.

'Ginger. I have always found the male form to be repulsive, but I must admit you are the most beautiful woman I have ever met. You have me so confused. I am so incredibly attracted to you.'

Her eyes appear appreciative as she speaks.

'How about we grow a friendship first, and leave anything else till after the operation?'

You heartily agree before encouraging her to lay on the bed with you. You hold her till she falls asleep. You soon follow.

END

79

You signal to the cute girl in an apologetic manner and indicate that you are going to talk to the DJ. The girl produces a mock pout and mouths 'come back' through the thumping music. With effort you struggle to the side of the stage where DJX is waiting. Taking you by the hand, DJX leads you to a backstage area. Here the music is muted slightly, making it easier to converse.

DJX, or Riley, as she asks you to call her, is incredibly happy to see you. She was shocked to hear of your breakup, but sort of knew it was going to occur.

'I'd seen you ex with someone else. I'm sorry.'

Noticing how sad the conversation makes you she asks about you and how you are feeling. She appears to show genuine interest.

'So, what have you been up to?'

You find conversation with Riley easy, and free flowing. She is nicer than you remember. When you had last met her, your ex was there, and for some reason, your ex didn't like her. Though you can't recall why.

'Would you like to join me for dinner? At my place?'

Do you choose to go home with Riley?
Turn to 40
Do you choose to return to the cute girl on the dance floor?
Turn to 55

80

Realising you just made a dick of yourself, by nearly falling, you approach the brunette. She blushes as you sit next to her. You introduce yourself and she introduces herself as Lucy.

'I'm sorry for laughing.'

She says apologetically before continuing.

'I did the same thing, and thought I was the only clumsy idiot on public transport.'

You joke with her.

'I'm an idiot?'

She appears sensitive and blushes with your comment. You apologise but she brushes it off saying you have every right.

You ask about Lucy's night and find out she's going to a homeless shelter to serve dinner. You admire her commitment. She asks about your night, but you find the idea of the club less ideal next to her charity work. You tell her the truth anyway. As Lucy talks about her charity work, you find her excitement contagious.

Her generous spirit is enviable. It makes you reflect on your life.

As you are talking, the bus pulls up at the club. A few drunk patrons enter the bus, via the front door. One, looks like she's going to throw up, but manages to stop herself.

Do you choose to enter the club?
Turn to 58
Do you choose to assist Lucy at the homeless shelter?
Turn to 68

81

You just manage to stop in time for the red light. A car that you had not seen rushes crossways through the intersection. You breathe a sigh of relief, knowing that if you had continued, you would have been in the path of that car. Your night would have been over before it had even started, if you had crashed. Possibly your life.

You look around while waiting for the light to change, when you see a police motor bike behind an advertising billboard. Wow, you think, if the car didn't get me then the police would have.

You are starting to think this is going to be a lucky night. How awesome. You can barely contain your excitement as you finally reach the club. You feel like you are ready for anything. Anything at all.

You enter the club.
Turn to 58

82

Though it's late, the idea of a movie with Lucy is appealing. You have a strong desire to spend more time with her and find out who she is. Like a couple of teenagers, you buy popcorn and frozen drinks, then head to the back row of the cinema. From there you throw popcorn at the noisy people in the dark and giggle hysterically.

You have a fantastic night especially when you make out, yet like a kid, you worry that people may be looking. It saddens you when the movie ends so you invite Lucy to breakfast at the local pancake house. She gladly accepts.

The next twenty four hours go by in a blur. You and Lucy explore the town like visitors, laughing and giggling all the way. Everything seems new and fresh. Time with her makes you feel adventurous and daring. Your ex is completely wiped from your mind.

Yet you know at some point Lucy may have to leave you. Or does she?

END

83

You tip the girl a hundred and give her a quick smile. She takes the money and turns to leave. You don't give her a second thought as you look towards the spa. The Swedish girls have now thrown bubble bath into the water and the bubbles are pouring out over the floor. The girls don't care as they rub the bubbles into each other's body. You gulp, and step forward in anticipation of the night's events. The room service girl grabs your arm. You turn to her. She informs you that the room is rented to a mobster who is due back in town soon.

'How soon?'

She looks at her watch and then tells you about ten minutes. It is his money in the jar and he has told the girls to wait for him. In fact, he owns the soccer team. The girl says he isn't fond of others 'playing' with his girls.

You thank her for the information and admit it might be best to leave. She tells you the girls aren't looking so if you get some cash from the jar, you and she can have a good time in one of the vacant rooms. Taking her up on the offer, you dash to the jar, grab some loot and hand in hand head out the door, giggling.

You don't regret your decision. In the morning, you hear the penthouse got raided and shots were fired.

END

84

You had been daring when you took the paper with your teeth. You were even proud of yourself for driving here and entering this room. But now, that you have seen the metal chest, you are starting to have doubts. You had been known to be a little wild in your youth, breaking a few rules.

Nothing though, had prepared you for what you'd seen in the chest. No, you're not a prude, but the chest was packed with toys and other items that looked like medieval torture devices. You feel way out of your depth.

Stepping backwards, you try the door, but it's locked. Officer Goode gives you a wicked grin as she drops the key into her pants. She's daring you. You have little choice other than leaping through the glass window or locking yourself in the bathroom. Unfortunately, you have a no self-harm policy and Officer Goode stands between you and the bathroom. Her look says she wouldn't take 'no' as an answer anyway.

Turn to 22

85

Maddie waves to you as you approach. The waitress she is talking to leaves before you get there.

'How's things?'

She asks though I bet she is surprised by your presence.

'Not bad.'

You answer as you scan the bar.

Maddie responds to your unsaid thought.

'Not too many in here but I saw a looker enter the dance club. And some soccer players enter the beer garden. What do you think?'

Not much takes your attention in the bar. You do see a red head in the corner, though red isn't normally your type.

Looking around at your options, which seem limited, you shrug towards Maddie.

'I'm not too fussed. Honestly, I mainly came to have a few drinks. What's your plan?'

Maddie looks as indecisive as you. That, or she had something else on her mind.

Do you choose to enter the dance club?
Turn to 3
Do you choose to approach the red head?
Turn to 2
Do you choose to buy Maddie a drink?
Turn to 90
Do you choose to enter the beer garden?
Turn to 61

86

Embarrassed, you admit you have never played with a sex toy before, let alone hold one. So, as to be honest, you explain to Ginger about the bathroom accident which led to the dong being in the bath tub. She laughs with you and admits she has never played with one either, though she is curious about them.

After a couple more drinks she suggests that the two of you go to the local adult store and pick a toy out. She looks timid in her request. Feeling light headed you say 'why not.' Hand in hand the two of you walk unsteadily to the local adult shop and enter via the back entrance.

The shop is brighter than anticipated, and the salesgirl more helpful than expected. The array of coloured toys makes you laugh. In the shop Ginger is loud, picking up toys left and right.

The salesgirl approaches you and says she might have something the two of you would like. She is holding a pot of green stuff and indicates to the change room.

Do you choose to follow the salesgirl?
Turn to 47
Do you choose to continue shopping?
Turn to 34

87

Yes, your old favourites have always brought you luck. You remember scoring way out of your league thanks to the Smurfs. The Italian model thought they were so adorable, she couldn't resist you, or the ten tequilas you'd bought her. Tonight you hope to let loose and if you happen to drop your pants, like the way you met your ex, you need winning underwear.

Thoughts of your ex fills you with disgust. If the Smurfs make an appearance, you hope she sees them and realise what she's lost. Thinking about lost, you dig in the back of your cupboard looking for the clothes you used to wear out. The ones your ex thought were a little immature, or unsuitable.

You realise now that your ex was always trying to change you and that she never liked who you really were. You throw on your old favourite jeans, surprised that they still fit. Glancing in the mirror you admire yourself before selecting a shirt. What look are you going for? Trying a few on, you wonder if you should look fun, adventurous or just flirty.

Do you choose a T-shirt?
Turn to 33
Do you choose a dress shirt?
Turn to 91

88

You are on a roll, so you decide to sing with the band. They make a song choice which, fortunately, you know. It's a little rockier than you're used to but you are keen to give it a go. The lead singer tells you to go for it.

The music kicks in and you soon follow. You leap around the stage like a crazy woman. The audience goes absolutely mental. The band plays harder so that you don't take all the limelight, but it's too late, you have it all. After that song the audience screams for more so the band kicks into another tune.

You don't know the words to that song so you make them up. The audience goes ballistic enjoying every moment. At the end of what feels like a long set, the band ask if you could tour with them. The lead singer admits that she prefers to be a backup singer because her voice doesn't have the vocal range of yours.

What a surprise. You didn't even know that you could sing that good. You accept their offer and spend the next six months touring with them. By the time the band signs with a major label, and you tour internationally, you have the most hits of any music website in history. Groupies attend every concert but you don't care as you form a committed relationship with your back up singer. You finally remember where you know her from. She was your dentist, who if you recall rightly, originally turned down a dinner date with you.

END

89

You offer to take Cassidy to the lake for the night. She looks at you for a moment, as if she was about to say no, but then she says yes, with a smile spreading across her face. You smile too.

The twenty kilometres to the lake is a pleasant ride. Cassidy loosely hangs her arms about your waist while her head rests on your back. The scenery changes from suburbia to lush green paddocks and then a vast body of water, sparkling in the moonlight. On arrival Cassidy spreads out a blanket she has in her pack. You both sit there on the water's edge. Unexpectedly, Cassidy leaps to her feet, strips, then streaks naked into the water. She splashes you till you join her.

You play like children in the water, splashing and duck diving. When the two of you finally drag your bodies from the water Cassidy throws you down onto the blanket and kisses you passionately. You return the kiss and let your hands wander across her fully tanned body. Cassidy allows you to roll above her, and she arches her back to press her body into yours. The thrill floods you with desire.

The two of you are passionate for many hours. You don't recall how many as you fall asleep. You lay lulled in Cassidy's warm embrace. It is not till a rumble wakes you that you realise Cassidy is no longer beside you. Sitting up quickly you see Cassidy, her pack and your bike heading down the road. You curse but it doesn't help. You just pray she left your mobile phone behind.

Do you choose to wait and see if she returns?
Turn to 77
Do you choose to start walking home?
Turn to 23

90

You ask Maddie if she'd like another drink and she looks at you strangely. You question the look.

'What?'

'Girl, are you flirting with me?

All you can do is laugh and jokingly respond.

'So what?'

She laughs too but gives you a different look to normal.

'Honestly, there's no action in the club tonight. Nothing worth pursuing.'

You look around, nodding in agreement.

'Yes, noticed that in the first five seconds!'

She asks if you want to go back to her place for a few drinks.

'Like when we were younger? Some alcohol, some gossip. You know?'

You agree to the idea, and head out with her.

It is fun reminiscing about when you were younger. How the two of you tried to start a band but both of you were useless musically. A few more drinks and out of the blue Maddie kisses you.

'Forgive me. I've had the maddest of crushes on you for the longest time. And you look amazing tonight.'

One thing leads to another, and before you know it you have both spent a wild night together. You've slept over before but it was never this enjoyable. In the morning you wake with a heavy head. To your surprise Maddie is awake and smiling at you.

Out of nowhere, your ex bursts through the door. She is yelling.

'You sod! How could you do this to me? I thought we made a commitment and now you're cheating on me. On me!?'

You are about to defend yourself when you suddenly realise she is talking to Maddie, not you. As she is yelling, you get up, get dressed and leave them to it. In your mind they deserve each other.

END

91

Yes, you feel a dress shirt gives a casual but classy look: seductive yet mature. It's been so long since you've gone out. No way you want to look like a scrubber. Yet you're still unsure of how easy to look, because no matter what, you want to get laid!

Grabbing a bottle of wine you pour a fairly large glass. You scull it quickly thinking how that would have annoyed your ex. You're actually happy to be drinking wine again instead of beer. Pouring a second glass, you flick off the music channel and check the news. Not much is happening in the world but you watch anyway while sipping your wine.

After a few moments you head to the bathroom. You are not big on make-up but a little makes you look fresh and alive. Applying the make-up carefully, you soon become bored with the task. After checking your hair, you head out to the entry way trying to decide whether to just take your wallet or a handbag. You make your choice before you realise you still have the wine glass in hand. You wonder how many glasses that was? Actually, you don't give a damn how many that was. Glancing at your watch you realise you are running a little behind schedule.

Do you choose to take a cab?
Turn to 21
Do you choose to take your new car?
Turn to 73

92

You offer your best rock star look and ask the room service girl to join you in the spa. You are standing in the water with the Swedish girls clinging to your legs. It's a shame you forgot your camera.

The girl politely refuses before turning away. It looks as if she is talking into something but you can't see what. Moments later a helicopter is hovering above you, its spotlight searching the balcony. The light stops as it focuses on you.

A herd of police charge through the door. The room service girl strips off her jacket, while holding up a detective's badge. She starts reading you your rights. The Swedish girls are pouting in the spa as the police take you away.

It takes most of the night before the detective believes you are not the drug dealer they are looking for. They apologise for the mistake, saying that they had the wrong hotel but the amount of money in the jar for tips was quite immense. And without a description of the culprit, other than they liked blondes, they just assumed it was you. The detective apologizes for ruining a night that looked sensational.

Do you choose to ask the detective out?
Turn to 18
Do you choose to ring the Swedish girls to pick you up?
Turn to 59

93

You wake up in your own bed. The morning sun glaring into your room. You rub the sleep from your eyes while attempting to remember last night. When you move the pleasurable soreness floods the memories back into your mind.

Last night with Officer Goode was the wildest experience you have ever had. She did things to you that you'd only ever heard of. Some not even that. You recall the pain but more strongly, you remember the pleasure. You lay in bed allowing the memories to flood your body so that it too can relive last night.

Once you feel settled enough; you switch on the television, mainly for background noise, while considering heading out to run another red light. The thought happily lingers when a news article takes your eye. It's about an increase in red light runners. The story goes on to reveal how a woman acting as a police officer is physically punishing those who are running red lights. Though none of the victims are willing to press charges.

Leaning back in the bed you marvel over the story before falling back to sleep. Your body is tired. Your dreams are full of Officer Goode. Not until you wake do you realise that you will never see her again. It's a sad, sad, thought.

END

94

You walk over and tip the room service girl two hundred dollars. You've always wanted to do that. She smiles in appreciation but you are looking at the Swedish girls who are still preoccupied with something else.

'There's more of that, if you know what I mean.'

You joke with the girl as you tap your pocket. She looks away from you and quickly leaves. You dart out of the room too and catch up with her in the lift.

She is quite gorgeous in a studious way.

'What's your name? It's late, will your shift be done soon?'

You joke with her that you will give her a hundred dollars if she leaves with you right now. Her cheeks become flushed. The lift jolts to a stop and the doors ding open. The girl darts off in another direction. You don't think much of it as you exit the foyer of the hotel. You ask the doorman to get you a cab.

When the cab pulls up, you open the door to enter, but are held back from behind. Looking around, a police officer is holding your arm. You panic as you think you will be charged with theft. Instead, the officer arrests you for solicitation. The room service girl is at the main entrance, one arm holding the concierge and the other pointing at you.

END

95

Though it's hard to admit, it's been a while since you exercised. The initial running around the park, chasing the Brazilians, leaves you puffing for breath. You blame the alcohol. To your disadvantage, the Brazilians are only semi drunk compared to your team which is practically comatosed.

A second wind hits, possibly the tequila, and you steal the ball. Dodging, you are passing players better than you could imagine. A Brazilian player slides, wiping your legs out. It's painful but you get a free kick at goal. You don't give up now. Though you've seen it on television, you've never shot at goal before.

Looking like you're going to kick one way you attempt to kick the other. The ball goes in neither direction, just straight down the centre. It's enough though, as the Brazilian goalie is confused and leaps sideways leaving an open goal for your slow rolling ball. You score and both sides go wild.

The Brazilians lift you onto their shoulders. Your leg is still paining as they carry you back to the bar as a champion. Everyone wants to buy you a drink, something you welcome, but the pain is becoming intense.

Do you choose to continue to party?
Turn to 57
Do you choose to get medical help?
Turn to 63

96

Yes, you think, a flash of a French lacy G-string is a sure-fire way to pick up. Sipping your glass of wine, you consider which colour to wear. Black is traditional and seductive. Red is wild. So, what does leopard print reveal about you? Considering the choices for a moment, you sip more wine.

Your ex always preferred you to wear boxers, though they were never truly comfortable to you. Nor did you find them as sexy as she did. Normally you wore something under them, or tried to only wear them about the house. Tonight, you could make your own decisions.

You look into the wardrobe glad that you have so much more space now. After she left you finally emptied the two cartons of clothes stored in the garage. They held the outfits you loved but she hated. It hits you now: she was always trying to dress you down. Such a thing was stifling: like your personality was being suppressed. So that leaves the decision for tonight open to your own discretion. How liberating!

Do you choose a dress?
Turn to 27
Do you choose jeans and a dress shirt?
Turn to 91

97

Cassidy leaps onto the back of your bike. She is quite weightless but her pack tests your balance. You wait for her arms to wrap around you before you take off for the bus stop. Her embrace is warm and firm. You like it. As you open up the bike through the straight, Cassidy rests her head on your back. You imagine her hair flying free.

At the bus stop, Cassidy leaps off the back and throws her arms around you in appreciation. You look at her and then your watch. The bus is still a half hour away. You feel for Cassidy, knowing how hard it is in a different country, or even in a different town.

You flick the kickstand, rise then dismount so as to stand with Cassidy, as you've decided to keep her company. She asks about the bike and about you. Laughing at her jokes, you realise how easy she is to get along with. Her sense of adventure inspires you and makes you realise what you have forfeited in life. The dreams left unpursued.

As you are waiting, Cassidy asks if you know of any cheap backpacker accommodation in town.

Do you choose to leave Cassidy and go to the club?
Turn to 58
Do you choose to offer Cassidy a place to stay overnight?
Turn to page 17

98

You figure that the club is only two stops away so you might as well stay standing near the front of the bus. Besides, the brunette up the back is still smirking.

As the bus pulls to a halt at the next stop, you are forced to take a seat. A group of athletic women enter the bus. They have matching tracksuits and strangely matching blonde hair. You find this amusing. One of them sits next to you while more sit in front and behind you. The conversation they started outside of the bus continues as they flow in.

The blonde next to you smiles. You smile back. She asks if you are from around here and you nod. Some of the others start talking to you. You discover that they are a visiting women's soccer team from Sweden. They have been training in some secluded spot for two weeks and this is their first night out.

You mention the club. Several appear interested in dancing. The blonde next to you and the two in front, do not appear to be as interested. They ask if you would like to join them at their hotel for some fun.

The conversation, and the women, have been so distracting that you realise the bus is about to leave the club bus stop.

Do you choose to go to the club?
Turn to 58
Do you choose to go with the soccer team?
Turn to 30

99

Millie talks passionately about her music and her potential career. Groupies, she says, are a side thing. The only benefit is that they come to all of your concerts so you are guaranteed a minimum crowd. Her laugh excites you.

You reach across the table and take her hand. In surprise, she snatches it back.

'I didn't realise that is why you asked me to dinner.'

You have the courtesy to look ashamed yet explain that you find her an amazing woman so dedicated to her dream.

'I was hoping that passionate energy would rub off on me.'

You say how lost in life you feel at the moment. Abandoned by those you thought loved you. Millie is sympathetic to your tale and suggests you are not like her normal groupies and laughs. You laugh too, totally smitten with this woman. The incredible energy she has draws you in.

She speaks freely for the remainder of the night

and chooses to sleep in your guest bedroom. You are initially saddened by this outcome for the night yet months later when you sell her sweaty stage clothes on eBay for thousands you feel vindicated. She even writes a song about you, which becomes a number one. Well at least you think it is about you.

END

100

Gently you approach the officer's breast with your face. The sweet smell of her makes you giddy. This is the closest you've been to breasts in such a long time. Carefully you place your teeth around the piece of paper trying not to nip any skin. That peachy goodness. Your tongue has a desire to dart from your mouth but you restrain it well.

Officer Goode bends down to peer through the window, she seems pleased with your actions.

'My, my, you are an adventurous one. How about you follow me to that address now.'

You can't believe the good fortune that has befallen you. You completely forget about Maddie who is probably looking after herself anyway. Plus, the aim of getting out tonight was to get laid. This most definitely seems the best and fastest way.

'Yes ma'am.'

Was all you could stammer.

Officer Goode smiles mischievously while returning to her bike. You check the address before the police bike roars into life and heads down the road. You attempt to follow but she is too quick. Lucky you have the address.

Do you choose to follow Officer Goode?
Turn to 52
Do you choose to go to the club?
Turn to 58

Tex Star

Though my name, Tex Star, is a pen name. Literally. I write because life is a journey full of the unexpected. My own has been intriguing, boring at times, and full of laughter. Nearly every moment expressed in one of my books has been experienced by me. Take note, I mean every one, even the embarrassing and absurd. Shocking hey?

Honestly, this fun book was written by me, for me, but you can read it too. As a child I was captivated by the Choose Your Own Adventure Books. Sadly, I only ever owned one, yet I re-read it a million times. It fascinated me immensely. As a writer, I decided to challenge myself: I wanted to write a story in the same manner the adventure books were written.

Admittedly, Big Night Out may not be a full 'adventure', but I think it works. No mountains are climbed, no rivers traversed, and no mountain bikes crashed. Maybe in the next one! Big Night Out plays on the ideal of getting back out into the world after a break-up. A time when one's perception on clubbing and dating may have been changed due to the lack of practice. Isn't that an adventure in itself? I think so.

I'm looking forward to experimenting more with these books. Seeing where the boundaries can take us.